Dragonfly

RESA NELSON

ISBN: 1507626207
ISBN-13: 978-1507626207

ACKNOWLEDGEMENTS

Many thanks to my fellow authors, Carla Johnson and Frank Stearns, who read this novel before publication and gave me excellent feedback.

Also by Resa Nelson

The Dragonslayer Series:

The Dragonslayer's Sword (Book 1)
The Iron Maiden (Book 2)
The Stone of Darkness (Book 3)
The Dragon's Egg (Book 4)

Standalone novels:

Our Lady of the Absolute
All of Us Were Sophie

CHAPTER 1

That's a lie.

Annoyed by the sound of her own voice inside her head, Greeta ignored it and focused on the task at hand. At Papa's request, she walked the beach every morning at sunrise and searched for driftwood. She remembered earlier days when he'd called her by her given name, Margreet. The name came from the lands far across the sea, the lands behind where the sun rose each morning. Squinting, she saw little but the sunlight sparkling across the calm waters. Greeta didn't know why she looked toward the homeland she couldn't remember or why it seemed to mean so much to her.

You long for the Northlands because

you'd fit in. You'd look like everyone else. You wouldn't be an outcast.

"I'm not an outcast," Greeta said. She faced the morning sun that skimmed the ocean horizon, grateful for its warmth on her bare arms and legs, the rest of her body covered in a buckskin dress, fringed at the knees. She listened to the music of the waves, lapping ever closer to her feet. She stood at the edge of the Bay of Oysters in the Crescent Valley, the easternmost part of the Great Turtle Lands. "I have a place in the Shining Star Nation and the Great Turtle Lands. My Uncle Killing Crow gave me my Shining Star name: I'm Dragonfly."

The voice inside her head laughed.

Dragonfly. A bug. A little bit of nothing. A thing you can squash with one hand. Everyone else in the Shining Star Nation has a name of consequence. Their names show strength and resolve and the cleverness needed to survive in this world.

How can a dragonfly survive without such people to protect her?

Greeta ignored the question and kept walking. She snatched bits of wood from the sand as if they'd offended her. "Don't talk to me like that. I'm a grown woman."

Truly? A grown woman?

"Other women my age have babies." Greeta bit her lip, wishing she could take back her words.

But you don't. You can't. And yet you call yourself a woman?

Greeta picked up her pace, ignoring the smallest pieces of wood she'd normally collect because she now decided they weren't worth her attention. "Auntie Peppa says I'm slow to grow. She says not all girls become women at the same time. She says for some it comes early and for others it can come very late. She says my time will come some day."

And yet you've had the body of a woman for the past few years. Face it, Dragonfly. It's even more proof that you don't belong here. You don't belong anywhere.

"I belong to the Northlands. I can always go home to the Northlands."

To a place that no longer exists?

Greeta reached the point where jagged rocks stretched out into the sea, blocking her path. She turned around and retraced her steps. "No one knows that. Not for sure."

For as long as she could remember, Papa had told her the story of how they came to the Great Turtle Lands with Auntie Peppa in a beautiful wooden ship shaped like a fearsome sea dragon. They described its long and wide overlapping planks, curving gracefully to shape the dragon's curled head and matching tail raised high and ready to strike while slicing through the icy waters of the great, wide ocean. Her father claimed they'd sailed from the opposite side of the ocean where he and her mother had been blacksmiths in a land full of dragons and brigands and ghosts. He'd been separated from Auntie Peppa for many years because she'd run away to seek safety in the Bog-lands, a place in the farthest North where she'd worked gathering iron to be smelted.

The way Papa told the story, when they'd landed here on this beach, Killing Crow waited in the tall grasses, ready to kill them because he believed they came to threaten the people of the Shining Star Nation. Papa said Greeta saved all of their lives that day because she ran on her toddler legs to Killing Crow and won his heart.

Of course, Killing Crow told the story differently. He admitted he'd witnessed signs that danger would come, and he prepared himself to defend his people. But he would look at Greeta with a reverence she didn't understand. He'd then say how remarkable and special Greeta was, claiming that she would someday hold a unique place in the hearts of the Shining Star people. Killing Crow would then wink and say what truly melted his heart was the moment he saw Auntie Peppa and knew he'd found the love of his life.

Greeta thought they all exaggerated her importance. After all, she'd been a little girl at the time. What could she have done that was so special?

Out of habit she touched the pendant she wore on a slim leather thong around her neck. All people in the Shining Star Nation wore a token representing their name. All tokens were carved from stone, but Greeta's was a combination of stone and silver. Papa had made a tiny sword from one of his silver rings he'd brought from the old country, half the length of her littlest finger. Uncle Killing Crow had fashioned and attached wings of stone to the sword, which served as the body of a dragonfly.

Tall grasses rustled on the small rise above her, and Greeta caught a glimpse of Wapiti, a man with long black hair and dark skin that identified all people of the Shining Star Nation and of the entire Great Turtle Lands. Her blood quickened, and she would have been overjoyed at the opportunity to see him alone and outside their village where no one could look at them with judgment. She pushed the taunting voice out of her head and reclaimed her thoughts for herself. *What if he heard me? What if he's starting to think I'm too peculiar like everyone else?*

"Wapiti?" she called out, but no one answered. Greeta watched the tall grasses wave back and forth until they became still. Wapiti knew she came to the beach every morning. Maybe he'd come to surprise her. And maybe he'd been surprised by the way she'd talked out loud to the voice in her head instead.

The voice she'd pushed aside moments ago crept back. *Don't get your hopes up. Wapiti doesn't want a girl like you. He has no use for someone with pale skin and paler hair. And why would he want a woman who stands so tall she sees eye-to-eye with him? No man wants that.*

Greeta stood silent. She couldn't deny anything the voice said. Next to anyone native to these lands, her skin looked sickly and her blond hair made her feel like an old one whose hair had turned white. Although Papa and Auntie Peppa shared her coloring, somehow they didn't seem to stick out. And the three of them did tower like trees above all others. Although Papa had chosen to live alone with Greeta, the differences between Auntie Peppa and Killing Crow had never seemed to matter.

Greeta didn't understand why she felt so different. Only that she did.

A hawk screeched high in the air above. Greeta looked up to see its tail flash orange-red in the sunlight.

"Brother Hawk," she said, a wave of excitement washing through her. Everyone knew that hawks were bearers of important information. "What tidings do you bring?"

The predator bird sailed above her head and glided over the ocean waters.

Greeta followed its path, noticing that

the sun had risen enough so that it no longer blinded her when she looked out to sea. That's when she noticed something unusual.

She stood still, taking in the sight, not sure what it was. Small and distant, it matched the size of her thumbnail when she held her hand against the horizon.

But she knew even from this distance it didn't come from the natural world. Whatever rested on top of the sea at the edge of the horizon looked like it had been made by mortals.

Even from this distance, she could tell it rested low in the water and appeared to be flanked by a beast's head and tail, curling high and ready to strike. It sparked a moment of elation, and Greeta thought she remembered circling herself around her father's arm like the tail of what appeared to be a dragon ship. But she shook the foolish thought away, wondering why such a thing would even cross her mind.

The back of her neck prickled in fear. If this thing could appear on the horizon today, it most likely had the ability to move across the sea.

What if it appeared here on the beach

tomorrow?

Clinging to the bits of wood she'd gathered, Greeta sprinted from the beach and through the thin forest leading back to Oyster Bay, anxious to warn them of what she'd seen.

CHAPTER 2

Greeta ran toward the edge of her village, relieved to see her father tending his fire. Back in the Northlands he'd been a blacksmith, but here in the Great Turtle Lands he'd found so little metal that he couldn't even make the tools he needed for his trade. Instead, he'd switched his interest to the Northlander ways of planting and tending crops, which had been a new concept to the people of the Shining Star Nation and earned him great respect.

Uncle Killing Crow stood by Papa's side, and they exchanged words in earnest. Auntie Peppa, wrapped from head to toe in blankets, sat on a stone close to the fire, seeming to warm herself.

"Papa!" Greeta stumbled from the woods

into the clearing, only now realizing the run left her gasping for air. "I saw something in the ocean. I'm not sure what it is."

Uncle Killing Crow stared at her, his face straining with worry. He reached down with one hand to steady himself against a log and then sat on it.

"There you are, my Pretty Girly Girl," her father said, speaking the language of the Shining Star Nation even though Uncle Killing Crow understood the Northlander that Papa and Auntie Peppa often spoke. He smiled, showing none of her uncle's concern. "What kept you?"

Greeta hesitated, taking a few deep breaths to clear her dizzying head before speaking. She knew her father had heard her. Pretending he hadn't was his way of keeping everyone calm. "I saw something strange in the ocean, and it stood right at the edge of the horizon."

Papa picked up a stick and toed the ground until the dirt softened beneath his foot. Handing the stick to Greeta, he said, "Show me."

Greeta worked quickly, before what she'd seen became any fuzzier in her head. She drew a straight line to delineate the sea from the sky. On top of that line she drew a long and squat shape like the homes made of logs in her village. On top of that shape and in the middle of it, she drew a large square.

Papa stared at it, nodding in recognition.

When she stood, he wrapped an arm around her shoulder and drew her into a close hug. "Well done, Sweet Girl. Well done."

"What is it?" Uncle Killing Crow said, his voice as worried as the strained lines on his face.

Greeta wrapped her arms around her father, feeling his voice reverberate in his chest while she pulled herself close to him. All her life she'd known nothing but the safety of living with him in their village. Even though she worried she didn't fit in, Greeta knew nothing bad would happen to her. More and more, her peers had distanced themselves from her, but she could always count on Papa, Auntie Peppa, and Uncle Killing Crow. What she'd seen on the horizon made her worry for the first time for her life and the lives of those she loved.

"Could be a Northlander ship," Papa said. "Could be something else."

Uncle Killing Crow stood and paced. "Then the shaman is right. Dragonfly's time has come."

Greeta felt startled, thinking of Auntie Peppa and how she'd said Greeta's time to become a woman would come one day. Could that be what Uncle Killing Crow meant? But then she realized what else he'd said. "What shaman?"

The figure Greeta assumed was Auntie Peppa stood, shedding her blankets to reveal a young woman of the Shining Star Nation. Instead of being pale like Greeta and her family, the young woman had the black hair and brown skin of all Shining Star people. Facing Greeta, the shaman said, "It is your time to come with me and walk in dreams."

Greeta responded the way she always did when people tried to tell her what to do. "I'd rather stay here with my father and gather firewood." She smiled sweetly although disingenuously. "But I thank you kindly for the offer."

Her father released his embrace and took a step away from Greeta.

Killing Crow faced Greeta. "The shaman has come from afar. She saw you in a dream. She found me when the sun came up and said she came in search of the tall girl with no color in her hair or skin."

"Maybe she means Auntie Peppa."

The shaman stood firm. "No. I recognize you. My gift is to receive messages from the Other Side and relay those messages. The time has come for you to discover your gift so that you may use it." The shaman extended her hands, reaching out to Greeta. "I am to be your guide."

Greeta stood firm. "I don't need a guide. I'm not leaving. I already have a gift: my family, my friends, my home. I don't need any more gifts."

Uncle Killing Crow cleared his throat and exchanged a worried look with her father.

"I do not talk of a gift that someone will give to you," the shaman said. "I talk of the gift you were born with. I talk of the gift you have to give to the world in order to make it better."

"Better?" Greeta said. "The world is just fine the way it is."

Liar. You're pretending to be happy living

in a village where you're shunned more and more every day.

Greeta ignored the voice in her head. "I'm not leaving."

The shaman's eyes glazed over, and she appeared to stare at something that Greeta couldn't see. "Darkness fell over the Great Turtle Lands when you first arrived, although none of you were responsible for bringing it. In fact, your arrival became our hope for finding this darkness and extinguishing it."

"Then Papa or Auntie Peppa should help you, because they are older and wiser," Greeta said. "I'm the last person you should ask."

"They have different gifts," the shaman said. "Your gift is the one needed to quench the darkness."

Frustrated, Greeta turned to face her father. "I don't have any such gift. I want to stay here with you. It's my time to find love and have babies. That's all I want: to grow our family and make the Shining Star Nation stronger and better because of it."

The expression on her father's face surprised her. She expected him to glow with happiness. Instead, he frowned. "My Pretty Girly Girl. There's something we never told you. Something we hoped you'd never need to know."

"She has to know now," Uncle Killing Crow said. "She has to understand why."

Greeta didn't believe them. Papa wouldn't keep secrets from her. Why were they trying to convince her to leave? She spoke on impulse, telling them what she wanted to believe, something she hoped to be true. "I'm in love. I'm going to find him and bring him back to tell you that we're going to have babies. And you can't take a mother from her babies!"

Greeta dashed into the village, hoping to soon find the young man who could convince them they were wrong.

CHAPTER 3

The people of the Shining Star Nation lived in long and narrow homes made of logs. Sons lived with their parents all their lives, bringing their wives under the same roof to create their own additions to the family. Wapiti happened to be one son of many, and Greeta found his brothers mending a gap in the side of their house where part of a log had rotted away. Breathless from running, she slowed to a walk. "I need to find your brother."

Of all the families in Oyster Bay, this one treated her with the greatest kindness. Greeta suspected it might be because Wapiti had no sisters. She'd noticed trouble usually brewed among those of her own gender.

The eldest brother, Red Feather, supervised his brothers while they molded a mixture of mud and grass into the rotted space in the wall. Being the eldest gave him the honor of wearing his long black hair loose with one part of it braided: one braid signified being the first son. Following tradition, his brothers wore their hair tied at the nape of the neck. Red Feather welcomed Greeta with a warm smile. "Wapiti? Ditch him. That boy hasn't enough sense to appreciate the beauty of a butterfly that's landed on his nose." Red Feather winked. "Why not keep us company instead?"

For a moment, Greeta felt her heart flutter. Despite being the eldest of seven brothers, Red Feather stood the shortest and appeared the weakest. He paled in comparison to his siblings. And yet every time he looked at her, Red Feather seemed to gaze directly into her heart.

Greeta shook it off. Wapiti had been her dearest companion for as long as she could remember. Together, just the two of them, they'd ventured outside the edge of Oyster Bay as small children, exploring the mysteries of the marshes and the majesty of the ocean. Together, they'd discovered every field and valley surrounding the village. Wapiti had been the one to encourage her to be bold and adventurous. By the time they were five years old, he'd won her love and loyalty.

"Please," Greeta said. "Tell me where to find him."

Normally, Red Feather would have shrugged off his suggestion with good nature and answered her question. Today, the expression in his eyes flickered with worry. Glancing down at his eavesdropping brothers, all of them watching and listening instead of working, Red Feather gave the nearest one a scuff on the head and told them, "Get back to it!" Grumbling, they obeyed and returned to the task at hand.

Red Feather walked to face Greeta. Although he'd reached his full growth ten years ago, like most people of the Shining Star Nation he stood only as tall as Greeta's shoulders. Without warning, he took her hands in his and held onto them tightly. "Stay. I could use a friendly face this morning." He smiled, but even his smile seemed laced with apprehension.

"And even better when that friendly face is so beautiful."

Startled, Greeta pulled her hands out of his. Red Feather knew how she and Wapiti felt about each other. Everyone knew. How could Red Feather be so callous as to speak to her in such a suggestive way behind his younger brother's back?

How could he be so disloyal?

Startled, Red Feather's mouth gaped in surprise.

His next-eldest brother placed a careful hand on Red Feather's shoulder. "If we don't let her learn the truth, it's a cruelty. Greeta doesn't deserve that. Don't we owe her more than that?"

Red Feather closed his eyes and exhaled slowly. He nodded but kept his eyes shut.

"What truth?" Fear clutched at her. She felt like a bird struggling to fly out of hands trapping her in place.

Red Feather looked up at her, opened his mouth to speak, but stared at her in silence. Finally, he looked down at the ground, avoiding her gaze.

"Wapiti has gone to help Animosh check the nets for fish," the next-eldest brother said.

Greeta frowned. Her cousin Animosh had a baby to care for. Why would she be checking to see if any fish had been caught in the nets?

And why would Wapiti help her?

"Don't tell anyone where I've gone," she said. Still frowning, Greeta slipped away, heading toward the shallow bay full of fishing nets before her family and the strange shaman could find her.

CHAPTER 4

Greeta ran along the well-worn path on the upper side of the marsh standing between her village and the ocean. Although it might allow her family and the shaman to catch up with her if Wapiti's brothers went against her wishes and told them where she'd gone, she knew this route to be the fastest to the bay.

She had to find Wapiti. For years they'd danced around the idea of becoming wife and husband. They'd talked about moving Greeta into his family's house and daydreamed about having children of their own.

But during the past year, Wapiti had pulled away from her without explanation. The conversations about spending their lives together happened less and less. Greeta hadn't noticed his eyes wandering elsewhere, so she'd assumed he wanted to make sure of his decision before committing to it.

When she came to its end at a sand cliff, she stopped instead of following the path's curve to the left that wound around the cliff and led to the beach. From here she'd be able to spot Wapiti and Animosh anywhere in the bay and catch their attention by waving.

She first noticed the calmness of the sea. The incoming and unusually low waves approached lazily, announcing their presence with barely more than a splash instead of their typical booming thunder that often filled the beach. Greeta wrinkled her nose at the strong pungent smell of a sea creature that must have died and washed up on shore.

But she didn't see Wapiti or Animosh anywhere on the sand or in the shallow waters of the bay. Instead, she noticed one of the nets on the sand, barely visible from the edge of the cliff.

Greeta crept closer to the edge. A few clumps of tall grass grew along its edge, but sandy cliffs were unpredictable and constantly changing shape at the whim of the wind and the constant beating of the ocean waves. One wrong step could send the sands shifting and loosening enough to send her spilling over the edge. Although the fall would be short, it could be enough to harm anyone who took the tumble off the cliff's edge and onto the beach below.

A few feet away from the edge, she dropped to her hands and knees, walking on all fours until she saw Wapiti and Animosh directly below. Greeta waved, but they were too engrossed in conversation to notice her. She called out but a large wave crashed at the same moment, drowning her voice. Before she could try again, a flock of screaming gulls flew past, making it impossible to be heard.

Greeta hesitated, surprised by the way Wapiti posed and pranced in front of Animosh. Once the gulls had flown far enough away, Greeta realized he was making her cousin laugh.

What were they talking about?

Greeta lowered herself to lie on her belly. She cradled her chin on her folded arms. Guilt tugged at her. The people of the Shining Star Nation held one principle dear: to ask themselves how any decision will impact the next seven generations before making that decision, whether large or small. Uncle Killing Crow had taught this principle to Greeta by demonstrating how to put oneself in the shoes of others and consider their feelings before speaking or acting. Out of habit, Greeta asked herself how she would feel if Wapiti and Animosh were hiding and watching her.

Wapiti ignored you this morning. Don't you remember catching a glimpse of him walking past without acknowledging your presence? Does he still deserve your consideration?

The sea became quiet again, and Greeta could hear Wapiti when he spoke.

"I'm not an outcast," Wapiti said, exaggerating his voice and making it sound higher. "I have a place in the Shining Star Nation and the Great Turtle Lands. My Uncle Killing Crow made it so." He crossed his arms and pretended to speak to the empty air in front of him. "My Uncle Killing Crow gave me my Shining Star name: I'm Dragonfly." He stamped his foot for emphasis.

Greeta felt as if a rogue wave had come from nowhere and slammed her in the face, leaving her gasping for air and tumbling head over heels in the water, not knowing which way was up. Wapiti had repeated the words he'd overheard her speak out loud this morning. But he acted as if he were making fun of her. Ridiculing her.

Animosh cackled like a hen, slinging a winding-root net over her shoulder. "I told you so! That girl is crazy. She's nothing but trouble."

Stunned, Greeta stared over the cliff's edge at her cousin, making sure she hadn't mistaken the young woman for someone else in Oyster Bay. They'd grown up bound by ties of friendship, not just family. Animosh had always been Greeta's closest friend until she married Ozawa. Greeta knew his family disapproved of her, but surely they hadn't influenced Animosh so much that she'd break a lifelong friendship without a word to Greeta.

Wapiti gave Animosh a sly look and asked the question in Greeta's head. "How can you say that about your own family?"

Animosh scoffed. "Does she look like family?"

Her words cut into Greeta's heart. With a Northlander for a mother and a Shining Star man as her father, Animosh had mixed blood. She'd inherited her mother's Northlander face with a small nose and rounded cheekbones, unlike the Shining Star people whose profiles looked like jagged cliffs. She'd inherited her father's small stature as well as his dark hair and eyes. In winter, her skin paled several shades lighter so that her coloring stood halfway between that of her parents. But by mid-summer, like now, her skin darkened so that she looked like any other member of the Shining Star Nation.

Unlike Greeta, although Animosh was different, she had a way to fit in.

Wapiti shrugged. "So Dragonfly doesn't look like you. She's still your cousin. And she's my friend."

"But look at what she's done!" Animosh walked toward him. She took her time, swaying her hips from side to side, successful in drawing his attention to them. "First, she promised me she'd watch my children yesterday and never showed up."

Greeta's mouth gaped open, too stunned to speak. *I never promised her any such thing!*

Animosh continued, drawing closer to Wapiti with every step. "And last week when Mama had my children here on the beach, Dragonfly came to help but walked away and left them alone by the tide. They could have been swept out to sea! My babies could have been gone forever!"

"That's not true!" Greeta stood, now so angry that she'd found her voice. She towered above them on the edge of the cliff. "That's not what happened!"

Below, her cousin and friend looked up, Animosh with a smirk on her face and Wapiti with surprise and pain in his eyes.

"Are you challenging me?" Animosh said, crossing her arms and standing her ground.

"I'm calling you a liar." Greeta's heart sank, grateful that the rest of her family wasn't here to witness her accusation. "I helped Auntie Peppa that day. She had to step away for awhile and left me with the girls right there." Greeta pointed at a flat spot on the wide and open beach below. "When I gave the girls some berries, a flock of gulls landed by us and tried to take the berries from them. I stood between the gulls and your babies. Those birds tried to peck them. I protected them!"

Animosh pointed angrily at Greeta. "And the waves came in over them. You let my babies get hurt!"

"The tiniest bit of water lapped over them. They got a little wet. No harm done."

Animosh jabbed an accusing finger at Greeta again. "Don't ever come near my children again! You're incompetent. Thank the spirits you don't have your own children, because you'd ruin them."

Greeta caught her breath, stunned into silence that her own cousin would say such a thing.

Animosh gave Wapiti a knowing look. "Let's hope the men in this village have the sense to make sure you never have children."

Greeta prided herself on being a peaceful woman with a calm demeanor. But now all she wanted to do was punch her cousin in the face. Before she realized it, Greeta found herself racing down the path from the cliff to the beach. Once there, she drew upon all her willpower to keep her distance from Animosh, re-membering at the last moment that words could be more powerful than fists. "Why do you hate me so?"

Animosh smiled sweetly. "I don't hate you, Cousin. I want what's best for all. Don't you?"

"Of course, I do. But why do you tell lies about me?" Greeta blinked back tears, now feeling more hurt than angry. "Why are you making me out to be such a monster?"

Darkness passed through her cousin's eyes for a moment, and then she broad-ened her smile. "I tell the truth. You are the liar. And I'll do anything to protect my family and my people from liars."

Forgetting her pain, Greeta cried out in rage and lunged at Animosh, taking a swing at her.

Wapiti held onto Greeta's shoulders, keeping her out of fighting distance from her cousin. "Stop," he said in her ear. "You're better than this."

Animosh studied them and cocked her head to one side. "I'll even protect your father. You're such an embarrassment to him."

Still holding onto Greeta, Wapiti said, "Animosh! Enough!"

Greeta spoke before she could think. "Papa? How do you think I embarrass him?"

"Everyone knows there's something wrong with you. Even your father. I've heard my papa and mama talk about you. They say you're so different you could bring harm to Uncle. How he could suffer because of you. How he's been protecting a secret about you all your life." Animosh grinned. "He's even protecting you from that secret. He won't let you know what you truly are because you'd be so disgusted with yourself that you'd run away." Animosh snorted her disgust. "But you should leave. It would be the best thing for everyone. Sooner or later everyone will find out what the secret is. It's a bad secret. Bad enough to get your father banished. Do you want him to wander the country alone? How long do you think before a bear or a wolf had him for supper?"

Greeta stared at Animosh and said, "That's just another lie."

Animosh smirked. "Look at you. Chasing after Wapiti like a rutting animal. Don't you understand? You embarrass him."

Greeta noticed the change in Wapiti's touch on her shoulders. He still held her back, but his grip loosened and his hands trembled. She could have broken free easily but kept still instead, hoping his grip would become firm and strong again.

It didn't.

"No man will have you," Animosh continued. "You're an embarrassment to our people."

Angered by the weakness she sensed in Wapiti's hands, Greeta broke free and turned to face him.

Startled, his eyes widened when he met her gaze. He looked away to avoid it.

Greeta swallowed hard, her belly twisting and turning until she felt sick. How could this be happening? Wapiti had been her dearest friend for as long as she could remember. He was her ally. Her confidante. But now he stared at the ground as if he couldn't bear to look at her. "Wapiti," she said, hearing the heartbreak in her own voice. "Tell me you don't believe this."

He glanced up for a brief moment and shrugged. Wapiti looked back at the ground, stubbing at it with his toe.

Greeta turned and took a few steps back so she could keep them both in her view. "Why are you doing this?" she asked Animosh. "You already have a husband. You already have children. Why is it so important for you to make sure I can't have what you have? What have I ever done other than be your family and friend?"

Animosh blanched, looking unsure and startled. She regained her composure quickly. "The Shining Star Nation is my family. And my loyalty is to them." She took a deep breath. "Father says when the men from the Wetlands tribe came trading last month, they saw you. At first they thought you were a ghost. When Father explained who you are, they said you were an evil spirit. They thought you had cast a spell over us. It took all day for Father to convince them you're harmless. If he hadn't, they could have brought war on us."

"That can't be true," Greeta said. "Papa would have told me. Someone would have told me."

Animosh shrugged. "Maybe they know you don't want to hear the truth."

Turning toward Wapiti, Greeta said, "You believe her? You believe all her lies without questioning her? Without asking yourself why Animosh would make up such wicked stories?"

Wapiti kept staring at the ground. He showed no response, acting as if he hadn't heard her.

Greeta's voice cracked with pain. "When did you stop being my friend?"

"I'm still your friend," Wapiti said. He glanced up but kept his gaze on the ocean, not looking at either woman.

"Friends stand up for each other," Greeta said. "Either you're not my friend or I never knew you're a coward."

Wapiti shifted his gaze toward her, his eyes blazing. "I'm no coward."

Greeta felt a spark of hope. She knew how persuasive Animosh could be. Maybe the ugly stories she'd made up about Greeta had confused Wapiti.

What if she could prove to him that Animosh had told him lies? Greeta could win his loyalty back by taking him to the people who could straighten out this mess. Auntie Peppa, who could tell Wapiti that Greeta had indeed protected Animosh's children, allowing no harm to come anywhere near them. Papa, who could make it clear that he kept no secrets from Greeta, and that no secrets about her existed. And Uncle Killing Crow, who could vouch that no one had ever called Greeta an evil spirit or believed she'd cast a spell on the village.

Greeta hesitated, remembering the shaman woman who desired to take her away from Wapiti and Papa and Oyster Bay. If Greeta took Wapiti to her family in order to dispel Animosh's lies, then she risked encountering the shaman and her demands again.

But the shaman might provide even more proof for Wapiti. What was it the shaman had said?

It is your time to come with me and walk in dreams. The time has come for you to discover your gift so that you may use it. Your gift is the one needed to quench the darkness.

Evil spirits didn't have gifts to quench whatever darkness the shaman meant.

How could Greeta be an evil spirit? The shaman would prove it.

And once Wapiti understood Animosh had told him nothing but lies, it would be safe for him to proclaim his love for Greeta and make it clear they needed to marry and have babies of their own.

Greeta felt a deep sense of calmness wash over her. Stepping forward, she took Wapiti by the hand.

He flinched but allowed his hand to stay inside hers.

"There's an easy way to learn the truth," Greeta said. "We'll talk to my family, and they will set everything straight."

The sound of Animosh's laughter startled Greeta.

"Be careful," Animosh said, grinning. "You may not like what they reveal."

CHAPTER 5

Greeta led Wapiti by the hand to the house of Auntie Peppa and Uncle Killing Crow, quiet since the day Animosh had moved into the home of her husband's family.

And yet cries from inside the house made of logs pierced the air. Moments later, a toddler pushed aside the bearskin covering the doorway. Even though her father was of the Shining Star Nation and half of her mother's blood belonged to it, the little girl displayed Northlander traits: paler skin, bright blue eyes, and hair struggling between black and blonde. She tumbled onto the grass. Taking the fall in stride, the little girl righted herself back onto her feet and took a few more steps.

Letting go of Wapiti's hand Greeta knelt, throwing her arms open. "Brook!"

The toddler's face lit up at the sound of Greeta's voice, and she giggled, taking a series of precarious steps toward her.

Before the little girl could reach Greeta's open arms, Animosh called out, "Stony Brook!"

Startled, Brook took another tumble onto the soft grass. Although more gentle than her first fall, she burst into tears, crying as if her world had fallen apart.

Greeta noticed the way Brook looked at her with sorrow in her eyes. With a start, Greeta realized she understood that sorrow. The pain she saw in Brook's eyes matched her own fear when she thought about how her dearest ally, Wapiti, seemed to be slipping away from her. "Oh, my darling girl," Greeta said, stepping toward Brook, her arms still open.

Animosh swooped in and picked up Brook as if she were a pile of clothes needing to be laundered. "Keep your hands off my child." Her eyes squinted with jealousy and hate.

Tread with care. How would you feel if you had babies and you saw how they loved Animosh? How would you feel if you thought your own babies loved Animosh more than you? How will what you do next impact the next seven generations of your people?

Greeta crossed her arms and retreated one step. "I meant no harm. She's my blood, just like you."

Careful. Don't forget Stony Brook looks more like you than her own mother.

Before Animosh could respond, Greeta said, "But of course I'm just her mother's cousin."

Animosh pressed her lips together in a thin line, looking placated for now.

Auntie Peppa pushed aside the bearskin, holding her other grandbaby on her hip, and called for Stony Brook. Now Auntie Peppa pressed her lips in a thin line, mirroring her daughter's expression. Walking to face her daughter, Auntie Peppa handed Brook's younger brother to Animosh, who struggled to hold onto her thrashing little girl with one arm. "Take your children home to your husband," Auntie Peppa said, her voice dark and dangerous. She seemed to struggle to compose herself when she looked at Wapiti, but her tone remained calm. "Keep your hands off my daughter. Warriors do not steal what belongs to a brother warrior."

Wapiti froze as if surrounded by hunters.

"He's not a thief!" Greeta cried out before she could think through her words. "Blame Animosh for throwing temptation in his face."

Anger flamed in Auntie Peppa's eyes, but before she could respond Wapiti said, "Stay out of this, Dragonfly. It is not your concern."

Knowing his words to be true, Greeta struggled to be quiet and studied Wapiti, anxious to see how he would respond to Auntie Peppa's accusation. Greeta could see him thinking. Like everyone else in the Shining Star Nation—with the most likely exception of Animosh—he silently weighed his decision about how to respond, considering how his actions at this moment would affect all living now and their future descendents.

"It is true," he finally said. "Brother warriors must respect each other." Wapiti nodded his agreement with Auntie Peppa before he turned and walked away.

Struggling to balance a child on each hip, Animosh said to her mother, "You have no right to interfere! I'm a grown woman…"

"Then act like one," Auntie Peppa said. She pointed in the direction of Animosh's home. Anger flared in her eyes.

Animosh shrank the same way she had in childhood when she'd been caught doing something she shouldn't have. Hitching her children up higher on her hips, Animosh hunched over in defeat and walked away.

Greeta stood still, not knowing what to do. Her heart broke at the palpable disappointment she saw on Auntie Peppa's face, wanting to embrace her aunt and comfort her. At the same time, every claim that Animosh had made ran through Greeta's mind. She wanted to ask Auntie Peppa if anything Animosh said was true. Had men from the Wetlands tribe thought Greeta to be a ghost? Had they called her an evil spirit placing a spell over the Shining Star Nation? Had Uncle Killing Crow had to convince them otherwise to prevent war?

And what about the other claims Animosh had made?

Did Auntie Peppa and Uncle Killing Crow truly believe Greeta was so different that her presence in the village could bring harm to Papa? That he could suffer because of Greeta? That he'd been protecting a secret about Greeta all her life? And would that secret make Greeta disgusted with herself? Would she have to run away to protect her father from being banished if others found out about that secret?

Greeta didn't know if she had the courage to ask all those questions.

"Come here, child," Auntie Peppa said. "You're not to blame."

Greeta stepped toward her, wrapping her arms around her auntie and holding her close. "I need to ask you some questions about things Animosh told me."

Auntie Peppa gave her one more squeeze before stepping back and placing her hands on Greeta's shoulders. "Not now. There are more important questions we must address."

Greeta saw Papa step out of the darkness of Auntie Peppa's house and onto the shaded ground behind her. "No," Greeta said. "I need you to tell me the truth."

CHAPTER 6

Inside Auntie Peppa's house, Greeta settled down in its one large room, sitting in front of the hearth fire that needed tending after reducing itself to embers during the night. The scent of cooked Brittle Blossoms and Crackle Grain lingered in the air. To calm herself, she picked up a nearby stick and poked the fire into better flames. "Why would Animosh tell me these things if they aren't true?"

Papa and Auntie Peppa sat across the hearth from Greeta while Uncle Killing Crow paced behind them. "She envies you," Uncle said.

"She said she heard you and Auntie Peppa talking about men who came here from the Wetlands tribe. They saw me and thought I was a ghost. They said I was evil and had the Shining Star Nation under a spell."

Greeta expected her family to protest. She expected them to say the thought of her being evil was outrageous and that no men visiting the Shining Star Nation had ever said such things.

Instead, Papa and Auntie Peppa stared into the fire and Uncle Killing Crow kept pacing, scowling with worry.

Greeta felt as uneasy as Uncle looked. Gathering up her courage, she said, "If there's something wrong with me, just tell me."

"Ain't nothing wrong with my Pretty Girly Girl," Papa said, perhaps too quickly.

Greeta asked the question that had felt like stones weighing heavy on her shoulders for as long as she could remember. A question she'd asked many times but never heard an answer that satisfied her. "Why won't you tell me about my mother?"

Auntie Peppa rushed to answer before Papa could speak. "There's nothing to tell other than what you already know."

Uncle Killing Crow stopped pacing and stared at his wife. "Think of your words.

How they will help or hurt the next seven generations."

"I am." But Auntie Peppa crossed her arms and refused to meet his gaze. To Greeta she said, "Your mother disappeared before we left the Northlands. She knew a great war was coming, and she wanted you to be safe."

Greeta caught her breath. Auntie Peppa had just provided a new variation of the story the family had told for all these years. No one had ever mentioned a war before, only that Greeta's mother had responsibilities to others and after meeting those responsibilities she would board a Northlander ship to sail to the Great Turtle Lands. Someday, Papa had promised, she would find them and they'd be a family again.

"A war?" Greeta said. "Does that mean she's a warrior?"

"An Iron Maiden," Papa said, his voice both wistful and bursting with pride.

Iron Maiden?

"What does that mean?" Greeta said. Her heart pounded so hard she felt it everywhere, pushing from her chest through her arms and legs, tingling in her hands and feet. What had her mother been?

Auntie Peppa rushed to answer. "It's just a name someone gave her. Your mother was a blacksmith like your father. It's nothing you don't already know."

Greeta ignored her auntie and paid close attention to Papa. He squirmed and seemed distraught. She never knew how he'd act when she asked about her mother. Sometimes he grinned and told stories that made them both laugh. Other times his answers were clipped and sharp, his eyes welling with tears that told Greeta he felt too pained to talk about her missing mother. Wanting to ease whatever pain her father bore, Greeta had asked less often until she reached a point where she trusted Papa to bring up the subject of her mother.

But things had changed this morning. Animosh claimed she'd overheard conversations between her parents about Greeta being so different that people from other nations thought she was evil.

"The time has come for you to tell me the truth," Greeta said. "Why am I different? How am I different?" She addressed her uncle, thinking him the most likely to be honest with her. "Did you have to convince another nation that I'm not evil to keep a war from happening?"

Uncle stood still and looked directly at her. "Yes."

"No!" Auntie Peppa said, jumping to her feet. Her voice grew high pitched with panic. "There isn't a speck of evil inside you, and we are at peace with all nations."

"That is not the question Dragonfly asked," Uncle said, his voice soft and calm. "The girl is correct. She deserves to know the truth."

"Ain't for you to decide," Papa said. Still seated, he stretched out his legs in front of the hearth.

Greeta believed she saw a myriad of emotions run across her uncle's face, from frustration to anger to resolve to respect.

After taking and releasing a long breath, Uncle Killing Crow said, "I will go outside and leave you to talk."

Watching him leave the room, Auntie Peppa took Papa's hand and asked him, "Should I stay or go?"

Greeta didn't realize she was speaking until she heard the words come out of her mouth. "Go."

Papa and Auntie Peppa turned to her in surprise.

Greeta sat still and said nothing, not wanting to let them know she felt just as surprised that she'd answered a question she hadn't been asked.

Papa squeezed Auntie Peppa's hand and then nodded, letting her go.

Auntie Peppa walked away, leaving them without saying another word.

Papa stared into the fire. "You always been my dearest Girly Girl. Sometimes I think I love you more because you are different. Because it means you're like her."

Greeta took a breath to steady herself. "You're talking about my mother."

Papa nodded. He looked up at her, grinning. "She's a handful. Feisty. Willing to take no guff from no one. Breaking rules. Always running off, telling no one. Worrying us all. Making me mad."

Her mother was a rebel? All this information spun in Greeta's head, dizzying her. "She ran away? Where?"

Papa's smile grew wistful. "Where she could do the most good."

Again, Greeta spoke before she realized it. "Is that why she left us? Is it why I don't remember her?"

The expression in Papa's eyes turned grim. "She did it for reasons bigger than us."

Greeta felt as if she'd been punched in the gut, her insides twisting with pain. "How can a mother abandon a baby?"

The grimness in Papa's eyes became fierce. "She left you in my care. I done my best. Protected you with my very life every step of the way."

"I understand, Papa. I do. You wouldn't abandon me. But she did, and I don't understand it." Greeta heard the passion rising in her voice. "I'd give anything to have children, and I could never abandon them. I'd love them and take care of them. I'd be like you–I'd protect them with my life. I don't understand why my mother wouldn't do that for me. What's wrong with her?"

The expression in Papa's eyes flared like the flames in the hearth fire between them. "Speak no ill of your mother!"

His anger startled her. Papa rarely lost his temper, and when he did it happened for good reason.

But a new purpose overwhelmed Greeta and gave her the courage to speak. "All these years I've had questions I didn't want to ask because I see how much you love her. How much you miss her. I never wanted to hurt you by pushing you to talk about someone who hurt you so much."

Still angry, Papa said, "She never meant harm to me. Or you."

"Then why isn't she here? Why did she stay behind in the Northlands?"

Now Greeta could see the decisions weighing in Papa's head roll across his face. "Please, Papa," she said. "Tell me."

He weighed his words as carefully as his thoughts. "I made an oath not to tell. It was a condition for the privilege of keeping you as my daughter."

An oath? A condition? Nothing Papa said made any sense. Unless he wasn't her kin.

"Are you saying you're not my father?"

He gave her a sharp look. "Never doubt I'm your father. By blood and by birth-right."

Now Greeta felt confused. "If you're my father, why would you have to promise my mother that you'd never tell me why she left us?"

"I made no such promise to your mother," Papa said. "Your mother never met you. She doesn't know you exist."

CHAPTER 7

Greeta stared at her father in astonishment. "That's impossible. How can any woman not know she gave birth to a child?"

The wood in the hearth fire between them crackled and popped, causing a flame to flare violently.

Instead of answering Greeta, Papa stared at the fire and leaned away from it as if in fear. "I said too much." He looked across the hearth at her, sorrow drawing the light out of his eyes. "Tell no one what I said. For your own sake and mine."

Animosh's words haunted Greeta.

Everyone knows there's something wrong with you. Even your father.

He stood, turning to leave the room.

"What's wrong with me?" Greeta said.

"Nothing," Papa said. "Everything is all right with you. It's the world that's wrong." He paused and corrected himself. "Not the world. The people in it."

Greeta jumped to her feet, circled the hearth, and stood between her father and the door to the outside world. Here, they were alone. Here, they had privacy. Here, she had the best opportunity to get answers. "Why won't you tell me the truth?"

She expected him to be startled by her question, but he spoke as if talking about gathering berries or hauling water from the stream that ran by the village on its way to the bay. "I made a promise long ago. A promise that matters. I make no such promises lightly."

"But I'm your family. Your daughter. Your one child."

"There are two types of people," Papa said. "One type does what they have to for the sake of their family."

Animosh's accusations rang in Greeta's head.

I've heard my papa and mama talk about you. They say you're so different you could bring harm to Uncle. How he could suffer because of you. How he's been protecting a secret about you all your life.

"The other type does what they have to for the sake of the world and all its people."

He's even protecting you from that secret.

"You have to decide what type you are," Papa said.

He won't let you know what you truly are because you'd be so disgusted with yourself that you'd run away.

Greeta didn't understand. For as long as she could remember, she'd dreamed of having her own children and being the mother to them that she wished she'd had for herself. She wanted Papa to be a grandfather. She wanted to make their family bigger and make her own life more joyful. "What is there to decide? I already know what type of person I am. I will do whatever I must for the sake of my family."

Greeta expected Papa to laugh or smile or at least hug her close and tell her he agreed with her. Instead, his gaze fell away, and his body sagged in disappointment.

Sooner or later everyone will find out

what the secret is. It's a bad secret. Bad enough to get your father banished. Do you want him to wander the country alone? How long do you think before a bear or a wolf had him for supper?

Greeta steeled herself in her decision. Right now she had no children or husband, but she had Papa. Her loyalty to him stood fast. She would do anything to protect him and keep him safe, especially if he'd been doing the same for Greeta all her life. "Tell me the secret," she said.

"I can't," Papa said. He kissed her forehead.

"But you must. For both our sakes!" Greeta struggled to drum up an argument to convince him. "Why won't you tell me?"

Papa gave her a sad smile. "Because I'm the other type. And I keep the promises I make." He walked past her, and his shadow fell upon her when he pushed aside the bearskin covering the doorway and walked into the sunlight.

Greeta felt consumed by shame. She'd never imagined she and Papa could be so different, but now she knew he thought of her as his opposite because she'd choose to help and protect her own family instead of other people.

But why should she feel guilty? What was wrong with wanting to care for your own kin? It caused no harm.

Even so, Animosh's words continued to haunt her.

You should leave. It would be the best thing for everyone.

CHAPTER 8

Alone in Auntie Peppa and Uncle Killing Crow's home, Greeta stared at the hearth fire. The day had begun like any other only to fall apart. How could everything have gone so wrong so quickly?

Greeta thought about each step she'd taken this morning and tried to find meaning in it.

Like every morning, she'd walked the beach before dawn to look for driftwood to feed the hearth fire at home. Worries about being different—especially not yet having the ability to bear children— weighed so heavily that she'd talked out loud to the nagging voice inside her head.

That's when the hawk had appeared, its flight catching Greeta's attention and leading her gaze to the horizon where she'd seen what looked to be a ship in the far distance. The sight had filled her with dread and the insistent urge to tell Papa immediately.

She'd found Papa at their home with Uncle Killing Crow and a shaman. What was it the shaman had said?

It is your time to come with me and walk in dreams.

Although Greeta had initially brushed off those words, she now let them sink in. The shaman said Greeta had a gift, something to give to the whole world. The shaman claimed to be a guide. Did that mean she'd walk in dreams with Greeta? How could that be possible?

Greeta put those questions aside. Like the crops that Papa grew to feed their village, those questions were like a few stalks of corn growing among many in narrow rows. Papa always said you can't look only at one or two stalks to understand how well the crop is growing. Sometimes you must step far enough away to see how all the stalks grow together. Are some growing too slowly, overshadowed by others? Do they all seem robust or are some stalks spindly and weak? Everything you see will tell you what you need to know.

In her mind, Greeta took a step back and looked at this morning as if it were a crop of corn.

The shaman had upset her, because the last thing Greeta needed was to become even more different than everyone else in Oyster Bay. All other young women her age already had at least one child, and Greeta felt desperate to hold a baby in her arms. So she'd searched for Wapiti, believing he'd keep the promise he'd been making since they were children: to become her husband at last. But she'd found him with Animosh, ridiculing Greeta and believing her cousin's lies without hesitation.

"I don't understand," Greeta whispered to the empty air surrounding her. "Why wouldn't he stand up for me?"

Because he's not the man you think he is. He doesn't have the heart or the loyalty of Red Feather.

Greeta's thoughts startled her. Red Feather? Why should she think of Wapiti's eldest brother? She shook him out of her head.

She thought if she could take Wapiti to her family that everything would work out. Greeta had assumed they'd reveal the truth, set him straight, and that he'd finally understand the time had come for them to become husband and wife. Auntie Peppa had surprised her by ordering Wapiti to leave and then dismissing Animosh. When nothing went according to Greeta's plan, she'd demanded answers to the lies Animosh had told about her.

But they hadn't been lies. Not entirely.

Uncle Killing Crow admitted he'd prevented a war when visitors from another nation had seen Greeta and assumed she must be an evil spirit.

If Animosh had been right about that, didn't that mean she also might be right about Papa being at risk of being cast out of Oyster Bay because of Greeta? She couldn't let that happen. Greeta had no hesitation about doing whatever necessary to protect her father from losing everything and living in danger. The more she thought about it, the more Greeta realized the real possibility of the village rejecting him. So far, everything Animosh had told her this morning seemed to be true, including a secret to which Greeta had been oblivious. Papa had told her more about her mother this morning than ever before, and yet he refused to reveal a secret promise he claimed he'd made long ago.

A new thought occurred to Greeta.

What if there is another way to discover the secret that Papa says he must keep? What if you can find it by walking in dreams?

"The shaman," Greeta said aloud. "I have to find her."

CHAPTER 9

Greeta steeled herself, rising from where she sat in front of the hearth fire and thinking about how to approach her family. It should be simple: it boiled down to telling Papa and Uncle Killing Crow that she'd changed her mind about the shaman and needed to find her. They had encouraged her to follow the shaman, so she'd encounter no resistance from them.

Auntie Peppa? Under normal circumstances, Greeta would expect her aunt to protest. But after all that had happened this morning, she doubted anyone in her family would stand in her way.

A trace of guilt slid like a snake down her spine. Her family would assume Greeta wanted to follow the shaman for the reasons the stranger had arrived: to walk in dreams and discover the hidden gift she possessed. A gift the shaman said Greeta could use to better the world.

But that wasn't Greeta's intent. She wanted to learn how to walk in dreams because she thought it could help her learn the secret about her that Papa wouldn't discuss.

Greeta had to learn that secret. Animosh's words kept haunting her.

He won't let you know what you truly are because you'd be so disgusted with yourself that you'd run away.

If Papa wouldn't tell Greeta the secret about her true nature, she'd have to find another way to learn it. And if it meant letting her family believe her intents were for a more noble cause, so be it.

Greeta marched out of the house to see the shaman walking toward her family.

"Find anything?" Papa asked the shaman.

The shaman walked with a light gait, almost skipping like a little girl. "No." She paused to look at Greeta and smile.

The others followed the shaman's gaze, surprised to see Greeta emerge from the house where they'd left her. Auntie Peppa extended a hand, gesturing for Greeta to join them.

Greeta did so, purposely taking slow, calming breaths to help her think clearly. She needed to mind her words in order to keep her intent a secret.

The shaman watched her with the fierceness of an animal stalking its prey. She tilted her head as if listening. Moments later, she said, "No need to worry. Some do the right thing for the wrong reasons. Perhaps that is better than doing the wrong thing for the right reasons."

"What?" Papa said, frowning.

"Nothing." The shaman spoke with brightness in her voice. "Even though I saw nothing, it doesn't mean there wasn't anything there."

"I don't understand," Greeta whispered to Auntie Peppa.

"I went to see what you saw." Again, the shaman looked at Greeta with a disarming fierceness. "But I saw nothing on the horizon."

"It's gone?" Greeta said, the idea washing through her with relief. "It left?"

"Perhaps. Perhaps not."

Impatience tightened Papa's face. "Explain."

"Most of us see what we know. What we understand. Things we've seen all our lives and can identify." The shaman smiled. "The unknown can blind us. If something we cannot fathom appears, especially at a distance, it might as well be invisible for it is often impossible to see what we don't understand."

"Invisible," Papa said. The tone in his voice made it clear he didn't believe the shaman.

"Because we know not what it is?" Uncle Killing Crow said. "Then how could I see these three when they drifted upon our shore?"

"Your differences are slight." The shaman's eyes flashed with good humor. "Do you not know a mortal when you see one?"

Uncle Killing Crow caught his breath as if the shaman had questioned him about something he didn't want known.

Greeta stared at her uncle and saw panic on his face. At the same time she noticed Papa and Auntie Peppa had paled.

The shaman studied them for a few moments. She then cast her gaze at Greeta and winked.

Bewildered, Greeta felt the need to break the silence. "You're saying that Uncle Killing Crow could see us because even though we look different from his people, we're still people. Does that mean you couldn't see what I saw because it's something you've never seen before?"

"Precisely." The shaman nodded, encouraging Greeta to continue.

"So it's something I have seen before. I don't remember it, but I've seen it before."

"What you drew in the dirt," Papa said. "It looked like the ship we used to come here." He swallowed hard. "You were young. But you were on that ship. It crashed, fell apart. We washed on shore with bits of it around us."

Auntie Peppa perked up. "None of the Shining Star people ever saw our ship–only some of the wreckage that the waves brought in with us. So none of them would be able to see a ship that looked like it?" She turned to the shaman. "Including you?"

"Yes," the shaman said. "Now you understand."

Auntie Peppa took Greeta's hand and

reached her other hand toward Papa. "Then we should all go and look. Maybe we'll all see it."

"Perhaps. Except for the young one." The shaman pointed at Greeta.

The young one? Greeta thought. *That shaman looks no older than me!*

Papa took Auntie Peppa's hand out of Greeta's and into his own. He faced his sister squarely. "The shaman, she's come for Greeta. Says she can teach Greeta how to walk in dreams." Papa paused, and Greeta noticed how he squeezed Auntie Peppa's hands and searched her eyes. "This shaman says my girl's got a gift. Something that will help all of us. The whole world, she says."

Auntie Peppa stayed silent for a moment, her eyes going wide with a look that made Greeta think she understood what Papa meant. Once again, Animosh must be right. Auntie Peppa's reaction made Greeta believe that she and Papa had shared secrets for years, maybe even all of Greeta's life.

And that secret silently bound them together right now.

"I see," Auntie Peppa said, nodding her

understanding while still fixing her gaze with Papa. Brightening, she turned toward Greeta. "I believe you're on the verge of a great adventure."

Without knowing why, Greeta shuddered. "I don't want adventure," she said. "I want to be like you. I want to have babies and a husband. I don't want to go away."

"My Pretty Girly Girl," Papa said, his voice sounding sad and wistful.

Greeta knew that sound. He always talked like that when he knew she felt too timid to do something that would be good for her, even if she didn't understand that "good" until years later.

Auntie Peppa pulled her hands free and patted Papa on the shoulder before turning to Greeta. "Did I ever tell you about my adventure? The one before we all left the Northlands and sailed across the ocean?"

"Yes," Greeta said. "You used to be a Boglander. You gathered up bits of iron from the bogs and smelted them into blooms for blacksmiths."

Auntie Peppa nodded. "But did I ever tell you that I went there because I had to, not because I wanted to?"

Over the years, Greeta had heard many stories about her aunt's life in the Boglands, but she'd never talked about how she'd come to be there. Now she felt a keen interest to learn more. Maybe it would prove to be part of the secret Greeta needed to uncover about herself.

"Your father and I grew up and lived in the same village, of course. When I was your age I fell in love with a Midlander."

Greeta frowned. "Midlander?"

"The Midlands are just below the Northlands," Papa said. "And some of them fail to treat their women well."

"I don't understand." Greeta looked from Papa to Auntie Peppa, puzzled by why they looked so sad.

"He beat me until I nearly died," Auntie Peppa said softly.

"What?" Stunned, Greeta felt as if the world had come to a stop, freezing everything in time like a leaf on top of a pond turned to ice. "How can that be? Why would anyone do that?"

Uncle Killing Crow cleared his throat. "Not all people are like the Shining Star Nation. Many people don't know how to think about the next seven generations before they act. Some think of nothing but themselves."

For a moment, Greeta never wanted to leave Oyster Bay, not even under the guidance of a shaman. But she worried more about Auntie Peppa and what had happened to her. "What happened? Did Papa stop him?"

"He tried," Auntie Peppa said. "But I wouldn't let him. I loved my husband. Until I came close to death, I thought he loved me. I thought he didn't know how to treat me with love and believed I could teach him." Auntie Peppa shook her head in shame. "When I could walk again, I slipped away. I made my way to the Boglands, and that's where I found peace and safety. Being with them for many years healed me, body and spirit."

"But you called it an adventure."

Auntie Peppa grinned, exchanging a happier look with Papa. "It turned out to be a great adventure. The way it began was painful." Now she grinned at Uncle Killing Crow, who looked at her with the same kind of adoration he'd show to a goddess. "But the same adventure has brought me to wonderful places and led me to the people I love most."

Before Greeta could take another breath, Auntie Peppa stepped forward and embraced her.

"Including you," Auntie Peppa said. Then she whispered, "Be brave, little Dragonfly. I'm sure a wonderful adventure is waiting for you if you'll only find the courage to embrace it."

Suddenly, Greeta wanted to cry because Auntie Peppa's kind words made her understand the truth.

How could she be welcome in a village where her truest love and her own cousin betrayed her? How could she call this place a home when the people she trusted most had proven themselves callous and disloyal? Greeta realized she'd been fooling herself for her entire life. She was too different to belong here, and others could no longer tolerate her.

She believed the truth behind Auntie Peppa's gentle words was that Greeta had to find a new home where people could accept her.

CHAPTER 10

Greeta trudged behind the shaman, walking barefoot on moist sand that held firm beneath their feet. Sometimes the remnants of an ocean wave crept near them, threatening to lap over their toes but not quite making the required distance. Not long ago, Greeta had said her goodbyes to her family and left the only home she'd ever known. Glancing back, she considered turning around.

They'd all walked to the beach where she'd searched for driftwood earlier the same day: Papa, Auntie Peppa, and Uncle Killing Crow. Looking toward the eastern horizon, none of them had seen the peculiar sight that had stopped Greeta in her tracks. The sight that might have been a Northlander ship, so far away it had seemed to perch on the edge of the world. Even Greeta saw nothing but the ocean, making her wonder if she'd imagined it.

Maybe it had just been a sign that the time had come to leave Oyster Bay. Or like Auntie Peppa had said, that it was time for Greeta to have an adventure of her own.

And then Greeta remembered the proud look on Papa's face when he gave her one last hug, despite the tears in his eyes. The thought of disappointing her father made her cringe in shame.

Greeta forced herself to place one foot in front of the other, continuing to follow the shaman, who had chattered non-stop since leaving the village.

"Of course, it comes from my mother's side of the family. All the women walked with one foot in this world and the other foot in the Spirit world. Most are healers, but my mother and her mother were shamans."

When the shaman paused to take a breath, Greeta blurted out a question. "What's the difference?"

The shaman glanced back at Greeta. "Healers understand the medicine at our fingertips and how to use it. Shamans have the same knowledge, but we have a closer connection to the Spirits. That means we can be guides for mortals and messengers for the Spirits."

Greeta noticed that the shaman spoke seriously when she spoke about her responsibilities. But when the shaman had simply been chattering, she sounded like the girls in Oyster Bay. Greeta wondered if they could be friends. "What's your name?"

The shaman stopped, turned, and waited for Greeta to catch up. "Shadow."

When Greeta joined her side, Shadow walked next to her.

"Is it lonely?" Greeta said. "Being a shaman?"

Shadow gave a shy smile. "Sometimes. When I'm with people, they treat me with respect but they act like they're not supposed to talk to me any more than they have to. When I'm alone, the Spirits keep me company." Shadow's voice took a wistful tone. "It's easier walking in the Spirit world than the mortal one."

Greeta knew a little about the Spirit world, but she didn't know if she believed what she knew. It seemed strange to imagine another world that existed in the same space and time as the one she knew. Uncle Killing Crow had once described it as the way the ocean lapped near her feet right now: tide water rising on the shore in shallow, overlapping waves. Except the mortal world knew only of itself while the Spirit world saw and recognized each world for what it is.

At the same time, Papa and Auntie Peppa had told her stories of the gods from the Northlands, the gods of earth, fire, water, and air. Papa said the gods normally existed inside their element, invisible to mortals.

But sometimes, Papa said, the gods take mortal form and walk among us.

Greeta wasn't so sure about those stories either. They seemed awfully far-fetched.

Just as far-fetched as the thought of a Spirit world.

She liked Shadow and didn't want to offend her. And what if Shadow succeeded in helping Greeta walk in her dreams? Greeta had noticed that her dreams often revealed truths that had stared her in the

face but that she hadn't fully compre-
hended until her dreams made those
truths obvious. Maybe the secret Papa
kept had been staring her in the face all
this time, but she just hadn't dreamed
about it yet.

If Shadow could help Greeta walk in her
own dreams and find that truth, she'd be
willing to believe in anything.

Shadow resumed her chattering. "Most
Spirits I like. Some are my ancestors, and
I respect them. I'm grateful to them because knowing them makes me feel I know
where I come from. It's easier to know who
I am. How I'm like them and how I'm not.
Where my talents and thoughts come
from." She paused and gave Greeta a long
look. "Understanding your family goes a
long way toward understanding yourself."

Greeta became aware of her acute differences. She towered above Shadow like a
tree. Her skin looked pale and sickly next
to the shaman. Even though the sun's
rays were still weak at this time of year,
Greeta worried about getting burned because she typically spent most of the day
in the safety of the shade from the trees in
her village. "I'm so different I might as well

be an outcast. No man wants me. I thought I had friends, but they betrayed me."

Shadow nodded. "So we both feel alone in the mortal world."

Greeta drummed up her courage, hoping not to be rejected. "Maybe we could be alone together."

Shadow offered a cryptic smile. "Maybe."

Greeta took the shaman's response as a good sign. After all, hours ago the man she'd loved since childhood—the man she'd expected to father her children—had ridiculed and rejected her, and the cousin she'd trusted had stirred up Greeta's life into a hornet's nest. Already, Shadow proved to be a far kinder companion.

The women continued walking north along the beach all day, stopping every so often to eat what Papa had given to them, which the shaman carried in her pack. When the sun hung low, Shadow pointed at an odd-looking cliff rising in their path. "We'll stop here."

The cliff looked like a whale jumping out of the water with its nose pointed straight up toward the sky. It stood alone at the edge of the beach, seemingly rising out of the sand. Unlike the soft sandy cliffs lining the ocean's edge near Greeta's village, this one consisted of jagged rocks. Greeta followed the shaman, careful to step where she stepped. No one had to tell her that one false step could send her tumbling.

Near the peak, Greeta saw an opening in the rocks and followed Shadow inside to discover a small cave. The shaman knelt by a small pit surrounded by stones. Placing bits of brush and driftwood in the pit, she struck a flint with one of the small stones and started a fire. The heady, distinct scent of bumblebee bush filled the cave.

The flames lit the interior of the close quarters, and Greeta noticed carved images of animals on the stone walls surrounding them. One image startled her: a large lizard with a forked tongue. Before Greeta could ask the shaman about any of the images, Shadow reached into her pack and withdrew a handful of fragrant crushed herbs. She threw them onto the flames, and smoke emerged from the fire, rolling around their feet.

Shadow looked at Greeta and said,

"Sleep."

Before Greeta could respond, her world went dark.

CHAPTER 11

The darkness shifted and swirled around Greeta, making her feel as if a silent storm had infiltrated the cave, snuffed out the fire, and enveloped her. "Shadow!" she called out, terrified. Her voice rang in the empty cave. "Help me!"

But the shaman appeared to be lost in the storm.

Greeta reached out, trying to find a wall but feeling only air instead.

A clear, metallic ringing sounded in the distance, steady and rhythmical. Greeta turned toward the sound, comforted by it.

As suddenly as it had appeared, the darkness dissipated. The fresh light of a new day surrounded her, and Greeta found herself no longer inside a cave but outdoors on the edge of a village. Trees towered above, forming a forest behind her. Houses like none she'd ever seen dotted the open field of the village, shaded by clumps of trees. Houses that looked like angled roofs perched on the ground. The scent of roasted chicken and bread filled the air, making her hungry.

But all of this was impossible. The sun had set moments ago. How could a new day begin so quickly?

I'm in the Dreamtime, Greeta realized. *I'm walking in my dreams, just like Shadow promised would happen.*

Metal ringing against metal sounded again.

Scanning the village before her, Greeta noticed a flat stone roof raised on posts placed around a cluster of fires and blocks of iron. At one of those blocks, a man brought down his hammer, making the metal sing.

Anvils. Like the ones Papa told me about.

Greeta approached the place she knew must be a smithery and a large one at that. Because they'd found so little metal where the people of the Shining Star Nation lived, the most Papa had ever been able to forge were a small hammer and a few blades to prepare patches of earth for spring planting. He used a large, flat stone for an anvil. But over the years he'd told her many stories about what a true smithery should look like.

The man looked up from his anvil, sooty smudges covering his face. He smiled. "Welcome to Guell."

Greeta started with recognition. Papa had spoken of Guell often. He'd lived there with Mama. He'd also told Greeta many of the names of other people who lived in Guell. "Who are you?"

He returned to his work, swinging the hammer again. "Randim."

Greeta stared at him. Stories she'd heard all her life were beginning to materialize in front of her eyes. "I know you. My Papa used to work for you."

Randim grinned. "Trep. A good man." He winked at Greeta. "Tell him he's missed."

A sense of urgency overwhelmed Greeta. She didn't know how long she'd be able to walk in this dream or when it would end. She felt compelled to make the best use of her time. "I'm looking for my mother. You know her. I know you do."

Randim simply nodded, continuing with his work.

"I need to find her. Can you help me?"

Randim paused, letting the hammer rest on top of the metal he hammered while he looked at Greeta. He then used it to point over Greeta's shoulder. "She can."

Greeta turned to see a small woman in an open area swinging a sword that equaled her height. She'd tucked her auburn hair into a bun at the nape of her neck and the hem of her long skirt into her belt, exposing bare legs. Like Randim, she worked methodically, taking a slow and precise step with every sword strike at the empty air. Greeta kept plenty of distance between herself and the sword while approaching the woman. "Ma'am?" she called out.

The fierce look on the woman's face startled Greeta, but the fierceness melted into delight. Planting her feet in a wide stance, the woman staked her sword vertically into the ground. She held onto the pommel with one hand and beckoned with the other for Greeta to approach. Smiling, the woman said, "Every day I practice.

And every night in my dreams, I am the victor."

Greeta frowned, not understanding. She didn't remember anything that Papa had told her that would explain who this woman might be. Walking forward, she said, "I'm Greeta."

"Of course you are, my child," the woman said. "You are my namesake." She let go of the pommel, and the sword stood like a soldier next to her. The woman rested her elbow on top of the pommel. "I am Margreet, and your mother has asked me to look after you."

CHAPTER 12

Greeta felt as if she'd walked knee-deep into the ocean and an incoming wave had knocked her over. Excitement and anger and surprise rippled through her body. "My mother? Where is she?"

Margreet crossed her arms. She didn't appear to be much older than Greeta but acted as if she were. "That is nothing for you to be concerned about right now. There is a great deal ahead for which you must prepare. We have much to discuss." Margreet uprooted her sword from the ground.

Greeta caught her breath when she saw Margreet grab the middle of the sharp blade only to realize the woman's hands were gloved. "You don't understand. I've never met my mother. I grew up without her. I need her to tell me why she didn't come with me and my father."

Her face softened as Margreet sighed. "Your mother saved your life and your father's as well." Her tone sharpened. "How dare you be so ungrateful for that?" She gestured with her sword. "Now follow me!"

Struggling to keep up with Margreet as she took great strides through the heart of the village, Greeta said, "I'm not ungrateful." At the same time, she belatedly realized what her new mentor had said. "My mother saved our lives? How? And why didn't she find us afterwards?"

Ignoring her questions, Margreet forged ahead with long and purposeful strides, leading the way past the peculiar and tiny homes flanking the dirt path through the village. "First you must understand what lies ahead so that you may prepare yourself for it."

Under normal circumstances, Greeta believed in the importance of respecting her elders, even if the elder happened to be only a few years older, like Margreet. But wasn't this a dream? Didn't that mean

Margreet wasn't real? Everyone knew dreams boiled down to nothing more than imaginings in one's head while asleep.

And with these imaginings occurring in Greeta's head right now, she saw no reason not to take control.

After all, it was her head and her dream.

Greeta dashed ahead of Margreet and blocked her way. "I came here because I know there's a secret about my mother that Papa won't tell me. If I don't learn what that secret is, he could get hurt!" Greeta paused, thinking about what Animosh had said this morning. "What if he becomes an outcast? How would he survive? And it would all be because of me." Greeta drew herself up even taller, standing well above Margreet. "I demand you either tell me what I need to know or take me to my mother. Right now."

Margreet took a slow step back, gripping her long sword with both hands and pointing its sharp tip at the ground, looking ready to swing it up before Greeta could blink. "Do not speak to me of demands," Margreet said, her voice low with anger and speaking so quickly that

Greeta struggled to keep up. "How dare you condescend to one who has come to help you? To help you learn to protect yourself from the dangers that lie ahead?"

Shaken, Greeta stood her ground. "But this is my dream."

Margreet raised her sword vertically and then struck the ground with it, the tip coming within inches of Greeta.

The ground trembled beneath their feet, and a startled pair of mourning doves flew out of a nearby tree and toward the sky, their wings creating a gust that swirled around the women, raising leaves from the ground like the dead.

"Do not claim ownership of that which you have no understanding," Margreet said, her face flush with anger. "We have met in a space of dreams, but that doesn't mean this dream is one you own. Shame on you for your righteousness. Is it your desire to alienate all those who would help you?"

Seemingly out of nowhere, a crowd surrounded them. Greeta recognized the blacksmith Randim and other men who looked like they must work alongside him, based on the black smudges on their faces. Women with small children in their arms stood by their men.

Greeta felt her stance shrink, unable to hold herself high and proud. Looking at women who had what she didn't felt like an arrow to her heart. "I don't understand. How can this not be my dream?"

Margreet raised her sword and struck the ground again, raising a cloud of blinding black smoke. Lost in the smoke, Margreet's voice rang out like a hammer against an anvil. "It is a time of things that have transpired and things that will come to pass."

When the smoke cleared, they were no longer in the village but at a sea shore where night had fallen. For as far as Greeta could see, bonfires dotted the coastline, burning in the dark like the stars in the sky above. Greeta looked around to see women armed with swords and other weapons patrolling the shore. Looking out to sea, she noticed the faint outlines of ships like the one she'd seen on the horizon this morning.

"Don't you understand?" Margreet raised her voice until she nearly shouted. "There are still places in this world where no woman is safe. And if you fail to open your eyes, you are doomed to learn that lesson too late!"

"Please," Greeta said, scared by what she saw. "I just want to find my mother."

Margreet crashed her sword into the ground again. "Open your eyes!"

Crying out, Greeta obeyed. No longer in the Dreamtime, she found herself alone in a valley, surrounded by staggering mountains.

This is impossible. Shadow told me to sleep when we were inside a cave by the beach.

Greeta pinched herself. Flinching at the pain, she realized she had to be awake. This must be real. She spun, looking for the shaman and calling her name, only to hear her calls fall into silence.

She was alone.

CHAPTER 13

Panic-stricken, Greeta stared at the wilderness surrounding her. She stood in a small valley where the grass stood up to her knees. Mountains covered with pines surrounded her, their peaks rocky and barren. The heady scent of evergreens filled her head. The air tasted crisp and cool, even though the sun hung over the shoulder of the mountain to her right. Could it be mid-day even though she woke up only moments ago?

"I don't know where I am," Greeta said out loud, hoping that the shaman Shadow would pop out of hiding with a grin on her face at the trick she'd played.

But Greeta found herself alone. Her breathing grew ragged.

Where is Shadow? How could this happen? How is it possible? Did I walk when I was dreaming? Is that what she meant by walking in my dreams? Did she bring me here and then abandon me? Why would she do that?

A screech overhead made her look up. A large bird circled above, a silhouette against the sunlight.

"Sister Hawk!" Greeta called out, feeling hopeful. If Shadow had tricked and abandoned her, others might help her. "Would you be so kind to help me? I'm lost, and I need to find my way home."

The hawk dove at her.

Startled, Greeta cried out, covering her head with her hands and ducking into the grass.

The hawk skimmed the tall grass next to her, dipped into it briefly, and flew up with a mouse in its talons.

Awash with relief that she hadn't been the one attacked, Greeta stood and watched Sister Hawk take the meal to a branch of a dead tree on the edge of the valley. A fledgling hawk, almost as big as its mother, accepted the mouse and made quick work of it. Bits of baby fluff poked out among its sleek feathers.

"I didn't mean to interrupt your hunting," Greeta called out. "But I would appreciate it if you could find your way to help me."

Sister Hawk looked at Greeta and screeched before flying from the branch, along the valley's edge, and disappearing behind a mountain.

Greeta took heart. She waded through the knee-deep grass until she reached a stretch of dirt and rocks at the base of the mountain. Here, she saw a path winding between the mountains. Sister Hawk waited patiently, taking flight once more from the ground where she had stood.

Now Greeta could follow the direction of the raptor's flight, although she took her time picking her way through the rocky terrain. After several minutes she paused, listening.

She recognized the sound of rushing water. Could the ocean be so nearby, perhaps on the other side of the mountain?

Greeta continued picking her way between the small boulders and stones dotting the path, the sound of water be-

coming more pronounced as she progress-
sed. Finally, she rounded a corner to discover a river hidden between the mountains.

Sister Hawk screeched once more,
perched on top of a large boulder by the
river, a squirming fish caught in her feet.
The bird launched herself from the stone,
flying above Greeta's head.

"Thank you!" Greeta called, watching
the mother fly back to her young. She
made her way to where Sister Hawk had
perched and studied the river. Although
Greeta had never left her village until now,
Papa and Uncle Killing Crow often talked
about how the best way to find any village
is to follow a river. People need to live near
fresh water.

For a moment, terror gripped her,
making her feel like a fish caught in Sister
Hawk's talons.

*I don't know where I am. How far am I
from home? How do I get there? What if I go
the wrong way?*

Taking a deep breath to calm herself,
Greeta looked to her left. The river tumbled down as if making its way from
higher ground. Looking to her right, the

water continued on a downward slope.

There's no sense in going up the mountain. People are more likely to live beneath it.

With that thought, Greeta turned to her right and followed the rocky path alongside the river.

By mid-day, Greeta felt weary and frustrated. Although she wore deerskin shoes, the small stones forming the narrow path alongside the river made her feet hurt. The insistence of gnats and mosquitoes irritated her. Like all people of the Shining Star Nation, Greeta believed in honoring all forms of life, whether animal or plant or insect. The Shining Star people believed every life form had a lesson to teach, something from which mortals could learn and benefit. But she also believed in the right to protect herself should any of those life forms threaten to harm her.

She swatted a mosquito landing on her arm before it could bite her.

Greeta's stomach rumbled. She'd found a small patch of berries soon after discovering the river, but they'd satisfied her for only a short time. She'd never had much talent for fishing. Venturing into the woods made the most sense, though she didn't dare wander far from the river for fear of losing her way back to it. For now, she opted to keep walking.

Rounding a bend, she stopped short, startled by the sight of a black bear splashing in the middle of the river.

Panic seized her by the throat, but Greeta remembered what Uncle Killing Crow had always told her to do if she should encounter a bear. *Remember the bear's lesson: to look inside yourself as the bear does when it hibernates. Honor Brother Bear. Show him respect. And keep your distance.*

Greeta snapped back to her senses. The bear looked to be an adult with no cubs in sight. That meant it had to be Brother, not Sister, Bear. Had she encountered a female with her cubs, Greeta would have risked backing away and backtracking. Instead, she knelt to show her respect.

Minutes later, the bear trapped a large fish against a boulder in the river. The fish struggled, flopping and wriggling under Brother Bear's firm paw. He sat on his haunches, splashing loudly in the water, while getting a firm grip on his catch with both paws. Brother Bear bit the fish's head off, spending the next few minutes having a leisurely lunch. He then stepped out of the river, across its narrow shore, and lumbered into the woods.

Greeta stood still for a few minutes, listening to the loud cracks of wood that gradually became distant. Satisfied that Brother Bear had left, she continued, glancing at the point in the forest where the bear had entered.

The heady scent of berries caught her attention. Stepping toward the path Brother Bear had made, Greeta caught sight of a blackberry bush, heavy with ripe fruit. Grateful, she planted herself at the bush and ate her fill.

She wondered why Brother Bear left this bush untouched. Uncle Killing Crow loved telling the story about how he'd once encountered a bear sitting at a blackberry bush, happily eating.

Maybe the fish I saw Brother Bear eat was one of many. Maybe he'd had his fill.

Or maybe he sensed my presence and led me to the blackberries.

In either case, Greeta felt happy she'd met Brother Bear, especially because it hadn't been face to face.

She continued her journey throughout the afternoon, not used to walking on uneven terrain for such a long time. Despite her weariness and aching feet, Greeta pushed herself to keep walking. Finally, the woods crowding the river opened up to a field in front of her where she saw a woman carrying a pot toward the water. A young boy trailed behind, pausing to examine the grass along the way.

"Hello!" Greeta called out, excited to see another person at last. She hurried toward the woman.

The woman paused, holding on tight to her pot. Like all people of the Great Turtle Lands, she had brown skin and dark eyes and hair. The boy behind her perked up and waved. "Hello!" he cried.

Grinning, Greeta walked up to meet him. She remembered to use the name her village had given to her instead of her Northlander name. "My name is Dragonfly."

The boy stared at her in wide-eyed wonder. "I'm Tumbling Stone, but you can call me Stone if you want." He turned to face the woman. "Mama, look! She's pale like sand!" Looking at Greeta again, the boy babbled excitedly. "How did your hair get so white? Are you very old? And what happened to your skin? What happened to your color? Are you sick?"

"Tumbling Stone! Enough!" The woman took small steps toward him.

Greeta noticed the woman watch her with the same caution Greeta had used when she encountered Brother Bear earlier today. She decided to appeal to the woman's compassion. "I'm a member of the Shining Star Nation. I'm lost. I need help." For a moment, Greeta wondered if eventually she could find another village of people like this who might accept her and let her live among them.

"I'm good at finding things!" Tumbling Stone piped up. "Just yesterday an elder lost a tooth, and I found it so fast! He didn't want it back, and he let me keep it!" Glowing with delight, Tumbling Stone reached into his shoe and pulled out a broken, yellow tooth.

"Hush!" the woman said. Keeping her gaze fixed on Greeta, she said to the boy, "Go to the elder now. Tell him to come meet our visitor and bring others with him."

"Yes, Mama," Tumbling Stone said. Clutching the tooth, he raced away from the river.

"I mean no harm," Greeta said, worried about the woman's reaction. She thought it might help to ease the woman's concerns by introducing herself again. "My name is Dragonfly. When I was very young, my papa, my auntie, and I came to the Great Turtle Lands from far away. The Shining Star Nation welcomed us, and we joined them."

The woman adjusted her grip on the pot, now holding its rim like a weapon she could swing at Greeta's head if need be. But the harsh expression in her eyes softened.

Greeta considered running away because the woman's demeanor scared her. After all, Greeta's own cousin had claimed that when visiting men from the Wetlands tribe first saw Greeta, they thought she was a ghost. When Uncle Killing Crow explained she was a Northlander adopted by the Shining Star Nation, the Wetlands men said Greeta had to be an evil spirit that had cast a spell over her people. The woman and her boy must also be members of the Shining Star Nation because they spoke its language and their dress was similar to what Greeta knew.

Her feet hurt too much to run away, and she decided to hope for the best. Surely, members of her own nation would listen to her.

A man with long white braids approached, followed by several young men, all armed with chiseled stone knives.

Tumbling Stone skipped alongside them. "See? That's the funny one I was telling you about. I wasn't imagining anything. She's as real as you and me!"

Although the elder had straight white hair, he looked to be as healthy and almost as strong as the men with straight black hair who followed him. They looked startled, but the elder showed no surprise. He walked up to face Greeta.

When he drew close, his appearance shocked her. From a distance, he looked like any man of the Great Turtle Lands because of his dark skin and straight hair.

But now he stood close enough that Greeta could see that his eyes were as blue as her own.

CHAPTER 14

That evening Greeta sat in front of a large fire, surrounded by the entire Shining Star village that was not her own. Ever since encountering her by the river, they'd kept her at a distance. When she'd asked the elder why he had blue eyes like hers, he refused to reply and then vanished into a cave for the rest of the day, accompanied by a handful of men. When she asked others the same question, they shunned her.

Unlike Greeta's people, these villagers lived in a cave carved into the base of a sheer mountain wall, white rock rising straight toward the sky. A large fire stood like a sentry at the entrance, to which Greeta had not been allowed. A starless night sky hung above, and owls called to each other in the dark.

Greeta flinched at a sharp sting on her cheek and noticed a small and sharp-edged stone fall from her face to her lap. She held it up. "Who threw this?"

A little boy giggled and threw another, this time hitting her in the chest.

A woman sitting behind him looked to be his mother, and she placed gentle hands on his shoulders. "Are you thinking of the seven generations?"

Greeta let go of the tension in her body. She'd always been told that all people of the Great Turtle Lands practiced keeping the next seven generations in their thoughts before acting, but she'd also learned that what people say doesn't always turn out to be true. She felt a deep gratitude to the boy's mother for taking this moment not only to protect Greeta but to teach the child a lesson.

The boy pointed at Greeta. "I protect them from her!"

The woman's voice remained calm and patient. "And how are you protecting them?"

"She's bad. You can tell from her pale

skin and white hair. I won't let her hurt us. I make her see our strength." When the boy reached to the ground for another pebble, his mother wrapped her hands around his, preventing him from doing so.

"Does she not see our strength already?" his mother said. "Have we not captured her?"

Startled, Greeta said, "Captured?"

Now the boy's mother looked up at Greeta. Although seeming to speak to her son, the woman aimed a pointed look at Greeta. "Have we not already shown her that we are in charge? Doesn't she already understand that we have strength and she has none?" She released her grip on her son's hand and picked up the pebble he'd wanted to throw at Greeta. "Do you think she doesn't understand I could blind her with a single throw? And that if she tries to escape we will bring her down like a deer before she can run away?"

The boy sighed. When he spoke his voice trembled with disappointment. "I wanted to help."

The woman embraced him. "I see." She slipped the pebble into his hand. The boy's face lit up with glee, and he threw the stone at Greeta, who covered her face with her hands to protect it.

The elder and his men stepped into the light, waving those sitting closest to Greeta to move and make room so that they could sit surrounding her. The elder said, "We have determined this woman is who she says: a member of our Shining Star Nation."

Greeta felt relieved even though she believed she never should have been questioned at all. "Can you take me back home?"

Everyone became so still that the crackling of the fire seemed explosive in the silence. Finally, the elder spoke. "I am in charge of this hearing, and you will not speak until given permission."

Stunned, Greeta felt afraid of her own people for the first time. The elder's expression and tone gave her no doubt of the serious nature of the hearing. The absence of Papa and Auntie Peppa and Uncle Killing Crow and even the shaman, Shadow, made Greeta realize how alone and vulnerable she could be without them. She wondered again what had happened to Shadow. What if Shadow hadn't led

Greeta astray and abandoned her? What if something else had happened, something that put Shadow in danger? Maybe once the hearing ended Greeta could ask if anyone in this village had seen her.

"As always," the elder said, now addressing everyone in the village gathered around the fire. "We must begin by thinking of the next seven generations and how what we do here today will affect them."

A man with a face that reminded Greeta of a scheming badger sat next to the elder and spoke up. "The seventh generation is so far away, so many years away that it's impossible to know what their world will be like, although it could be that the world will be much like ours today. And so on with the sixth and the fifth. The only true participation we can have is from the first generation with us here today."

The words Badger Face said made no sense to Greeta. This wasn't how her people spoke of the seven generations. They never talked about what the future might look like for any generation. They never accepted input from the first generation because they believed that generation needed to be cared for, not consulted.

What kind of village is this?

"All members of the first generation arise," the elder said.

The children among the villagers stood. The boy who had thrown stones at Greeta smirked.

"You are the leaders of your children and your children's children," Badger Face said. "And they are the leaders of theirs. The decision we have before us will touch all of your lives and lives beyond."

Greeta shifted, growing more uncomfortable by the moment. *These people make no sense. Why are they asking children to act like adults? Why aren't they making good decisions to benefit those children instead?*

He gestured toward Greeta. "Tell us what you think of her."

"She's ugly!" the boy who had thrown the stones called out. "Look at her. She has no color, like some ugly bug that lives under a rock."

"She does too have some color," a girl standing taller than the boy said. She pointed at the elder. "She has eyes like him. The same blue eyes."

The boy scoffed. "She's nothing like him. Or like us. We should get rid of her."

The other children became wide-eyed, and many of them looked at the ground.

The elder cleared his throat. "What does the rest of the first generation think we should do with her?"

Some of the children looked up shyly, only to return their gazes to the ground.

"Speak up," Badger Face said.

"They're afraid to speak," the girl who had stood up for Greeta said. "They think he will hurt them later if they say anything different than what he says." She pointed at the boy.

"You do not have that fear," Badger Face said.

The girl drew herself up taller. "I'm bigger. He doesn't scare me." She lifted her chin a bit. "Scaring people into doing what you want is no way to honor the seven generations. It is shameful."

Greeta's spirits lifted. The girl spoke like a true member of the Shining Star Nation. She stood like a beacon among her people.

"This is not about fear," the elder said.

"No," Badger Face added. "Be afraid of

nothing except her." He pointed at Greeta.

"Then we should get rid of her." The boy kicked at the ground. "How many times do I have to say it?"

"Get rid of her," a much younger boy said.

Greeta looked at him, unconvinced that he understood the situation or what he'd said.

Other children chimed in. "Get rid of her!"

The girl tried shouting reason but the others drowned her out.

The elder stood, spreading his arms out and gesturing for quiet. "It is determined. We will make ourselves rid of her. But the question is how?"

Greeta cried out at the sting of a rock hitting her shoulder. When she looked up, she saw the boy grinning at her, an expression of triumph lighting up his face.

CHAPTER 15

The badger-faced man and his two companions led Greeta away the next morning, making her carry a satchel of food while they each carried a skin filled with water. She followed them past the base of the cliff to a path winding between mountain peaks. Although larger stones formed erratic steps, the ground between them was loose with pebbles. Greeta often lost her footing, and she stumbled to the ground a few times.

The men ignored her when she asked where they were taking her, but she persisted.

At mid-day they stopped halfway up the mountain at a juncture of two paths, one winding to one side and the second curving around to the other. Here, they were surrounded by jagged cliff faces, bare stone with pine forests growing above their heads. They seemed comfortable sitting an arm's reach from a sharp drop. One misstep would result in a long tumble off the mountainside to certain death. While the men drank from the skins they carried, Greeta edged away from the drop and clutched the satchel of food, determined to hold it hostage. "Where are you taking me?"

Badger Face reached toward her, gripped the top of the satchel, and yanked it out of Greeta's arms. He passed it to the other men, who withdrew strips of dried meat and small discs of bread. To Greeta, Badger Face said, "Where you can do no harm."

"Harm?" Greeta felt as if she'd been struck by a lightning bolt. She accepted a disc of bread, pausing to ask a question before devouring it. "What harm could I possibly bring to anyone?"

One of the men gave her a nervous laugh as if that would somehow answer her question. The man pointed to the path leading south at the juncture. "Your people have been weak. Foolish to keep you among them."

"My people?" Greeta said, her tone rising in astonishment. "They're the people of the Shining Star Nation. Just like you."

Badger Face scoffed. He plopped on the flat surface of a rock, sitting while he broke a meat stick in half before eating it. "We are Shining Star. But we're smarter than our brothers who live beneath us."

One of the men added, "Your people have easy lives, living by the sea. Their winters are simple and easy, while ours are harsh. They have a bounty of food, while ours is scarce and difficult to gather."

Greeta heard herself ask a question before she could think better of it. "Then why live here?"

The men's faces became tight and terse, making Greeta realize she should be more mindful instead of asking a question the moment it popped inside her head.

One man blurted, "Ask your elder!"

"She need not trouble herself with what has happened between her people and ours," Badger Face said, his voice as calm as a pond on a sunny winter day. "Where we take her, she will have no need to think of them again."

"She will think of them now!" a new voice cried out.

Greeta looked up and toward the sound of the voice, seeming to resonate off the mountain walls surrounding them. Three men stood in the bend of one curving path.

Red Feather and two of his brothers!

Greeta's heart split, rising at the sight of Wapiti's siblings and sinking at the realization he had not come with them.

Badger Face stood and spoke with continued calmness. "Who are you?"

"Her people," Red Feather said, walking toward them, tailed by his brothers. "We'll take her back home."

Awash with relief, Greeta stepped toward them, only to find Badger Face's firm grip holding her back. Turning to look at him, she saw hatred in his eyes.

"She trespassed into our territory," one of Badger Face's men said. "There is a price to pay."

Red Feather paused, now only a slight distance away, signaling his brothers to halt by his side. "But we're Shining Star

Nation," Red Feather said. "We're the same people."

Badger Face shifted his grip to Greeta's shoulder, tightening his hold on her. "Of course, we are." He extended his other hand in a gesture of welcome. "Come forward, Brother."

A sense of dread ran through Greeta's body, making her shiver. She caught Red Feather's gaze and shook her head slightly.

But Red Feather didn't take notice. Instead, he grinned, leading his brothers forward. "We've worried about her. If there's a price to be paid for any mistake she might have made, we can help pay that debt."

Before she could grasp what happened, Greeta found herself pushed onto the path, breaking her fall with her hands while witnessing Badger Face bend in one swift motion to lift Red Feather and hurl him over the mountainside.

Greeta felt as if the world had turned to ice, freezing her inside it. Before she could blink, the other men struck Red Feather's brothers, knocking them to the ground where they lay still.

"You killed them," Greeta heard herself say.

Badger Face peered over the edge of the cliff, looking down and nodding, grim satisfaction carving itself into his eyes. Walking over to examine Red Feather's brothers, he nudged each. "Only one died. These two still live."

Greeta scrambled on her hands and knees toward them, but Badger Face stopped her, bracing a firm foot against her shoulder.

To his companions, Badger Face said, "Make sure they will not interfere again."

The two men gathered long blades of thick grass and bound the hands and ankles of Red Feather's brothers, making it impossible to free themselves.

Greeta screamed.

With his foot still on her shoulder, Badger Face kicked her down to the ground.

"Why are you doing this?" Greeta said, feeling the world of ice shattering around her into dangerous shards. "Why would you hurt your own people?"

Badger Face's answer was short and simple. "The seven generations."

Greeta stared at him in astonishment. "The seven generations? But considering them is about keeping peace in the Great Turtle Lands. It's about prosperity for all and kindness and helping each other."

Badger Face shook his head. "Whoever told you that is a liar. Considering the next seven generations is about survival."

Greeta steeled herself. She had spoken the truth about the seven generations. If these people, these members of the Shining Star Nation, truly believed what Badger Face had just said, then they were crazy.

And very dangerous.

CHAPTER 16

Red Feather felt himself drifting as if rising out of a dream. The world swirled around him in a haze.

I'm dead. A man of the Shining Star Nation threw me over a cliff, and I'm dead.

He groaned, squinting at the bright sun overhead.

But if I'm dead, why does my body feel stiff and sore?

Red Feather assessed his surroundings. The sky spread above him. He found himself lying on top of a large mass of vegetation, bushes covered with large, soft leaves and bearing branches strong e-nough to hold his weight but gentle to the touch.

Sitting up, Red Feather kept mindful of

his body. He noticed a few scrapes and cuts on his skin. Bracing himself with his hands, he winced, picking up his left hand the way an animal favored its injured paw.

Something might be broken, but the pain isn't too great. I can manage.

Red Feather felt as if he were sitting in a nest created by a gigantic bird. The vegetation held him far enough above the ground that he had to wiggle to its edge and hop down. He winced when he landed, but only from an overall ache. Nothing had broken in his legs or feet. He realized he hadn't died, after all.

Now he could see the cliff behind him and the journey he must have taken on his fall down. The gentle bushes grew far above his head at the base of the cliff. His landing had compressed this section to a quarter of its size. These bushes had saved his life.

Like everyone in the Shining Star Nation (with the possible exception of the man who had thrown him over the cliff), Red Feather practiced a great respect for all living things. He believed all animals were his brothers and sisters. And he had an equal respect for all things green and growing. He placed his unbroken but cut hand on the bush that had cushioned his fall. "Many thanks, my friend. If not for you, I would have died."

A young leaf from the bush reached out and curled itself around his hand, as if holding it.

Startled, Red Feather stood still. When he and his brothers were young boys, their uncle would tell them stories of encounters he'd had with trees and plants. Uncle said they are more like us than we realize, and they respond in kind to how we treat them. Red Feather had believed those stories as a boy, but as an adult he assumed they were nothing more than stories meant to teach children how to walk in the world and be part of it.

The leaf clung to his hand, and slow warmth grew inside. That warmth spread up Red Feather's arm and throughout his body, easing the stiffness and aches.

Astonished, Red Feather spoke to the bush again. "You are a healing plant!"

The leaf squeezed his hand slightly as if in acknowledgment. It broke free from the bush, wrapping itself firmly around Red Feather's hand. He studied everything he noticed about the vegetation: its color, structure of growth, shape, and size. He wanted to learn its name and believed someone at home would know it.

Taking a step back, Red Feather bowed to the bush. "I thank you for your kindness and generosity."

The section of the vegetation that had been compressed by Red Feather's fall shook itself like a fox shaking off the rain and stretched back up to its normal height.

Red Feather watched it stretch, his gaze climbing the face of the cliff. A new thought struck him.

My brothers!

He didn't know what had happened to his brothers Monz and Nibi. They'd been standing behind him when he'd been thrown over the cliff. Could they have been thrown off, too?

Red Feather searched the base of the cliff, finding no bodies among the sharp rocks beyond the bushes. He called out to the vegetation. "Have you seen my brothers? Did any more like me fall?"

The tall bushes shook as if blown by a non-existent wind. Red Feather took their answer to mean no one else had come down.

Then he would have to climb up the mountain and look for his brothers. It would take far too long to walk behind the base of the mountain in search of the trails leading upward. Red Feather studied the cliff standing before him, rocky and sheer. For once he felt grateful to be the smallest among his brothers. He might not have the bulk and brawn of Wapiti, but Red Feather had the nimbleness to climb, finding it easier than larger men to discover and cling to narrow handholds and footholds.

Red Feather hesitated, considering all possibilities. His brothers might be dead. Or they might have been taken.

Or they might be injured and in need of help.

Facing the tall bushes again, Red Feather said, "I believe my brothers are hurt. Would you be so kind to help them as well?"

A breeze kicked up, shaking the bush in front of him until several leaves broke loose and landed at his feet.

Grinning, Red Feather said, "I thank

you once more." He gathered the leaves and tucked them under his belt.

Seeing a gap between the bushes lining the base of the cliff, he began his climb. He took his time, planning many steps ahead before taking the next. Most of the aches had vanished, but every so often he moved in a way that shot a twinge of pain through his body. He depended mostly on his feet and right hand, the left one having only two fingers that could hold a grip. The rest, he suspected, were broken. The sunlight warmed his back while the air grew cooler with every step. In the distance he heard the bleating of a mournful sheep.

Finally, Red Feather hauled himself over the edge of the path where he and his brothers had discovered Dragonfly and the strange men of the Shining Star Nation. He spotted his brothers slumped on the ground nearby and scrambled toward them to find out if they still lived. "Nibi!" he cried. "Monz!"

A tight ball of worry in Red Feather's chest broke free in relief when he saw his brothers stir and moan. They lay on the ground, and Red Feather saw their hands had been bound behind their backs with long grass, which he cut free with his knife. Their faces and hands were battered and bruised. Nibi had several shallow cuts on his forearms and the palms of his hands.

Red Feather retrieved the leaves and placed them on his brothers' wounds. "What happened?"

Nibi winced when the leaves adhered themselves to his cuts, not seeming to notice they were doing the work, not Red Feather. "Those men attacked us. They took Dragonfly." He paused, looking at Red Feather in wonder. "They threw you off the cliff. Are you a ghost?"

Red Feather smiled. "I think not." He gave Nibi a smart slap on the shoulder to prove his point.

Nibi scowled. "You didn't have to hit me."

"No, I did not have to hit you," Red Feather said lightly, turning his attention to Monz's injuries and treating them. "But considering your unabashed joy in discovering that I'm alive, I thought you might appreciate the proof."

Monz laughed while Nibi pouted. "Well

said, Brother," Monz said to Red Feather. "I'm overjoyed to see you alive. How did you survive the fall?"

Red Feather hesitated, applying the last leaf to a small gash on his brother's bloody forehead. He didn't want to start a debate about whether or not the bushes had communicated with him or wittingly saved his life. It was a story best told on another day. "I landed lucky."

"We're all lucky to be alive," Nibi said. "If we hurry, we could get to the place where we found shelter by dark. We'll be home by morning."

"Home?" Monz snorted. "And let those men who claim to be of the Shining Star Nation get away with what they did to us? It's our duty to make them account for the wrongs they've done. To make them pay!"

Red Feather studied the long grass he'd cut from his brothers' hands. If it had been strong enough to keep them bound, maybe he could make use of it for his own needs. He wrapped it around his broken hand, gesturing for Monz to tie the grass in place. "You're both forgetting about the seven generations. Think about the grand-children of the grandchildren of the grandchildren who will someday be ours."

"I don't even have a wife," Nibi muttered.

"Not the point," Monz said. "Pay attention."

Red Feather nodded his appreciation for his younger brother's respect. "If we do what Nibi wants and go home, we do not know what we're leaving behind. Who are these men? We know they will not hesitate to murder because they threw me over a cliff to certain death."

Nibi squinted. "Are you sure you're not a ghost?"

Monz smacked Nibi's head and then said to Red Feather, "Continue."

"What will happen if we ignore such people? What if their numbers grow? They might not harm us again, but what might they and their people do in the future? How might they harm the children of our children? The grandchildren of our grandchildren?"

Nibi sighed and looked away. "I don't know."

Red Feather gestured toward Monz. "And what if we go after them seeking them to account for their acts? Wouldn't such men fight back instead? And with their people behind them, might they not wage war against us, their own people?"

Monz grunted in agreement. "What else can we do?"

"Follow them without letting them know. Study them. And when the opportunity presents itself, take Dragonfly back home."

Monz met his brother's gaze. "You talk of stealth."

"That we hide like rabbits?" Nibi said.

Red Feather shook his head in disagreement. "That we stalk like wolves."

Nibi stared at Red Feather for a long moment. "She doesn't love you. Didn't you see her disappointment when she looked for Wapiti and saw he hadn't come?"

His brother's words stung like the bite of an insect. But Red Feather took no ill will. Nibi spoke from his own frustration of being scared and wanting to return home where he'd feel safe. This could be a moment to help teach his young sibling what it meant to be a warrior and have courage. "I understand. Do you think I should punish Dragonfly by abandoning her?"

"She isn't like us," Nibi said. "She isn't

one of us."

Monz smacked him in the head again. "And those men were? They look like our people. They speak our language. And yet they tried to kill our brother. If he hadn't found and freed us, we would have died, too!" Monz cast a look of disgust. "Dragonfly is more like us than those men." He hesitated, shifting his gaze toward Red Feather. "But the young one is right about one thing. You know she wants Wapiti, not you."

Red Feather nodded, seeing another opportunity to guide his siblings toward manhood. "Love is not about getting what you want from a woman. It is about what you can do to make her life better, whether she loves you or not. And right now what I can do is find Dragonfly and help her return to the family she loves." Red Feather stood, offering his good hand to help his brother stand. "Will you help me?"

Monz took his brother's hand and stood by his side. "Of course, Brother."

Nibi spent a moment studying them both. Finally, he scrambled to his feet. "I guess helping you is better than a smack in the head."

CHAPTER 17

Greeta followed Badger Face along the mountain path, his two companions bringing up the rear. Up ahead to the right and standing the height of a tree, water sheeted down a tall, slanted slope of rock, worn smooth and flat. Falling noisily onto a polished stone ledge below, the waterfall poured into a gulley and ran alongside the trail ahead.

They followed the stream on shallow banks made of stone covered with bright green moss. After traveling for a short while, the water rushed in a narrow stream between the towering granite walls standing no more than 12 feet apart. The walls looked like many layers of rocks had pressed into each other over the course of time, leaving jagged shelves and steps jutting out. Tiny plants grew from the crevices in the walls, slick with moisture. Water dripped from hanging vines.

How long had it been since she'd watched them kill Red Feather and then tie up his brothers, leaving them for dead? It seemed like an eternity while at the same time feeling as if it had happened only moments ago.

No one had ever warned Greeta that men could be capable of doing such terrible things. Until now, her life had been peaceful. Of course, Papa had taught her to not let anyone take advantage of her, and Uncle Killing Crow had talked of wars among nations. But wars rarely happened, and her corner of the Shining Star Nation had experienced no conflicts during her lifetime.

But murdering a man fell into a different realm. The memory of seeing Red Feather disappear over the edge of the cliff made her stomach turn.

It shouldn't have been Red Feather. It should have been Wapiti.

Those thoughts surprised Greeta. On one hand, disappointment that Wapiti hadn't come to help gnawed at her.

Wapiti didn't care enough to help you. He doesn't care about you. He cares about Animosh and doesn't care that she already has a husband and a child. He only cares about what he wants for himself.

The passageway narrowed even more, and Greeta trailed one hand along the granite wall to steady herself. When she'd first seen Red Feather, Monz, and Nibi, she'd looked beyond them hoping for Wapiti. Even though the appearance of three of his brothers had crushed her heart at first, her appreciation for them now overwhelmed her.

They cared enough to come looking for me. Red Feather must have been worried that I'd left with a shaman. Or maybe they received portents that something had gone wrong. They risked their lives for me. And now Red Feather has died and his brothers are still in danger.

The guilt that pressed down on Greeta made every step she took feel heavier.

Did Red Feather see the disappointment on my face? Was it obvious I wished Wapiti had come instead of him?

Greeta felt the hot embarrassment of

her tears when they streamed down her face, knowing it was too late to make things right with Red Feather.

But it may not be too late for Monz and Nibi.

Rubbing her face dry, Greeta considered what she could do. This narrow passageway trapped her between her captors: one walked ahead of her and two walked behind. But the passageway would end soon, most likely opening up to a wider trail. Lightweight and younger than the men, Greeta believed she could outrun them and make her way back to where they'd tied up Monz and Nibi. She could free them, and they could take her home.

A diversion would help her get a head start.

Several minutes later, the stream tumbled down a narrow slope filled with boulders, cascading over and around all sides. Up ahead, sunlight fell upon the treetops of tall pines with thin trunks.

The path branched in a few different directions through the mountainous woods. None of the men seemed certain about which direction to take.

"I need to pee," Greeta announced. She

spoke the truth while also thinking about how to use the act to her advantage.

Badger Face nudged one of his companions. "Go with her."

"No!" Greeta said, forcing herself to stand tall and firm even though fear made her legs tremble. "It isn't right." She pointed at a cluster of bushes near the mouth to the narrow passageway. "I can go there. I'll be close by."

Badger Face's men began to argue about which direction to take. Distracted by them, he waved his consent and then joined the argument.

Greeta took her time walking to the bush and relieved herself, making sure Badger Face could catch a slight glimpse of her presence when he glanced in her direction. She dawdled when finished, looking for a moment when the men were more engaged with each other than in watching her.

The argument grew more heated, and Badger Face turned his back toward her in order to point toward a branch in the path.

On quiet feet, Greeta slipped back inside the passageway. She walked a few soft steps and then broke into a run, small enough to gain good speed although the rocky walls on either side sometimes grazed her skin.

She heard Badger Face cry out, followed by hurried footsteps behind.

Don't panic. They're tall. They had to bend over just to walk through here. They can't run. They have to walk.

Soon Greeta emerged on the other side of the passageway, now facing the trail they'd descended. Quickly, she considered her options. Although the cliffs on either side no longer met, they still towered above her. She could either climb the trail or try to hide behind the sparse patches of bramble bushes, which provided enough cover for rabbit.

I can scramble up the path fast. It's my best chance.

Hoping she'd find a better hiding place along the way, Greeta hurried up the steep trail. She scurried along a mild incline and then dug her heels into a sharp rise of rocks, requiring her to use them like steps. They looked like the remnants of an avalanche.

Badger Face shouted in the distance,

his voice entombed in the passageway.

Reaching the top of the rock steps, Greeta faced an easier stretch of path, narrow but level and sure-footed.

She also spotted a large boulder that looked like it might have fallen away from the rest of the rocks that had avalanched.

Badger Face called out again, but this time his voice rang clear and closer. "Hurry!"

He's made it through the tunnel!

Terror overwhelmed Greeta, making her lose focus. She bolted toward the boulder, but her step caught a small rock, sending it flying and leaving a divot in the ground.

Most men in the Shining Star Nation were good trackers. Greeta rushed to retrieve the dislodged stone and put it back in place. She smoothed the wide streak her step had left in the dirt and then ran to the boulder and hid behind it, making certain every part of her body stayed low and out of sight.

A short time later she heard the men reach this part of the path. She squeezed her eyes shut and struggled to keep her breath slow and quiet.

She refrained from sighing in relief

when she heard footsteps continue up the path, away from her. If she could just keep hiding, sooner or later they'd give up. Or maybe once they'd traveled far enough up the mountain she could go down and take her chances running ahead of them.

Determined fingers dug into her shoulder and a strong arm wrapped around her waist, hauling Greeta to her feet. "She's here!"

If she hadn't recognized his voice, Greeta would have known Badger Face by the distinct stench he'd developed during the day. She tried to wrestle away, but his grip held strong. "Let me go!"

His companions returned from where they'd continued on the trail.

Badger Face dragged her back toward them, and the three of them surrounded her. "Listen well," Badger Face said. "With the way you look, it's clear there's got to be more at home like you. How easy do you think it would be for us to find them? You say you're of the Shining Star Nation, and we know every village, every tribe of our people. All we have to do is go back in the direction you came from. We'll ask along the way until someone has heard of you and your kind living with ours."

Greeta shuddered, not wanting these men to come anywhere near her family. "Don't."

Badger Face continued. "We will find everyone who looks like you, and we will kill them. Unless you stop trying to run away and do what I say."

"Yes," Greeta said, desperate to protect Papa and Auntie Peppa. "Whatever you say."

"Wait." One of the other men tapped Badger Face's shoulder. "Don't you think maybe he'll want them, too? The ones like her?"

All three men stared at her, seeming to consider her in a new light.

"Possibly," Badger Face said. "But it's not for us to decide. We take her to him, and then he decides."

"Who?" Greeta's curiosity replaced her fear. This was the first time anyone from this Shining Star village had mentioned someone specific. She'd assumed they were simply pushing her off on another tribe.

Ignoring her, one of the men said, "But he could use more like her."

Greeta didn't like the sound of someone using her and didn't want to put her family in danger. Right now everyone paid no attention to her questions. If she asked more, she'd draw attention to herself and possibly make them reconsider capturing Papa and Auntie Peppa.

No. I have to do whatever I can to keep them safe.

Badger Face grabbed her by the shoulders and gave Greeta a good shake. "Remember: try to run away again, we'll go after your people. Understand?"

Greeta nodded. Reluctantly, she followed him, wishing she'd never loved Wapiti. If she'd only seen him as a friend and nothing else, she never would have ended up in this mess.

From now on, I love no man.

CHAPTER 18

That night, the men built a fire at their campsite, taking turns to stay awake and watch Greeta to make sure she wouldn't run away again. But Greeta fell asleep quickly and soundly.

She dreamed she stood inside a large room, one hundred times larger than any home she'd ever seen and far more beautiful. Instead of dirt, the floor was made of flat, polished wood. Stone walls surrounded her. The ceiling stood as high as treetops.

"There you are," Margreet said, striding up to meet her with a pretty wooden stick in her hands. "You are late, and we have much work to do."

The woman's presence astonished Greeta. "But you're not real."

Margreet drew herself up in a huff. "I beg your pardon! I am quite real, and you will not exhibit disrespect by telling me I am not!"

"But—"

"No protests!" Margreet stood the stick in front of her. As tall as her shoulders, the wood looked as smooth and polished as the floor beneath their feet. It tapered to a point where it met the floor, but the other end had a round shape on which Margreet rested her hands. "I might not be alive like you, but I still exist. And I am here because your mother wishes for me to help you."

For the first time, Greeta noticed a woman at the opposite end of the room. Because of the grand size of the room, Greeta could tell little about the woman, especially because she kept moving in strange ways, swinging a stick like Margreet's through the air.

I must be in the Dreamtime! But how did I get here without Shadow to guide me?

"Once you find your way here the first time," Margreet said, "you can then do so by your own devices."

Her words startled Greeta, making her wonder if anyone else could read her mind while in the Dreamtime. She watched the woman at the other end of the room. "Why isn't my mother here? I want to meet her."

Margreet stepped between Greeta and the woman at the far side of the room, blocking the line of sight between them. "Because it is not yet time. You must learn to trust what I tell you. And the most pressing matter at hand is that you must learn to protect yourself from those who would harm you."

"Badger Face," Greeta said. "And those other men. They're taking me somewhere and I can't get away from them."

Margreet became still and quiet for a moment, briefly looking more like a shadow than a woman. "They are the least of your problems."

"But I tried running away. And they threatened my family. They already killed three men from my village. I can't let anyone else get hurt." Greeta felt helpless, letting that feeling overwhelm her. "There's nothing I can do to protect myself. I'm just a girl."

Margreet snapped back to herself, solid

and vibrant once more. "Nonsense!" She placed a firm grip on the polished stick and held it up. "This is called a waster. It is made in the shape of a sword."

Greeta brightened. "Papa told me about swords. My mama used to make them."

Margreet's face softened. "That, she did." Margreet regained her focus on the task at hand. "We train with wasters because if I taught you with a true sword you might kill me by accident."

Greeta frowned. "But if you aren't alive, how could that happen?"

Margreet stomped her foot on the lovely floor. "Don't ask such questions! You are only confusing the matter. You must never use a sword made of iron until you have learned how to use it properly. You could hurt yourself or other people. My point is that you must take responsibility for the way in which you train."

Responsibility. An idea hit Greeta with a jolt. "Three brothers from my village came to help me, but the men with me killed one of them and left the others to die. I have to help them! But the men said if I try to run away again, they'll hurt Papa and my Auntie Peppa. Can you help me?"

Margreet spread her arms wide, grazing Greeta with the waster she held in one hand. "What do you think it is I am trying to do now?"

Greeta frowned. "But there are no swords here. Papa's a blacksmith, and Mama taught him how to make special swords. But he says there's so little iron in the land that it would take a lifetime to find enough to make a single sword. So if there are no swords, then why should I learn how to use one?"

Margreet swung the waster up, letting the wooden blade rest on her shoulder. "I am not here to whittle away your time for no reason. Trust that there will come a day when you will see an opportunity to use what I am about to teach you. I am here to make sure you are ready to embrace the opportunity when it comes to you."

A chill ran through Greeta's body, the same as if she'd jumped into the cold ocean water. "But the brothers. If someone doesn't help them soon, they'll die."

"There is no need to worry about them." Margreet shrugged. "Everyone makes their own way in life, but everyone also has their own fate. Trust their fate. Trust your own."

Greeta wished Margreet had given her a better answer, but the petite woman scared her. Greeta could see her tolerance for answering questions grow shorter by the moment. She summoned up the courage to ask one final question. "You said you'll prepare me for an opportunity to use a sword. But how will I know the opportunity when I see it?"

For the first time, Margreet relaxed into a smile. She stepped close to Greeta and whispered in her ear. "Because you will hear me tell you so." Stepping back again, Margreet raised her voice to its normal volume. "Pay attention. Here is how you grip the sword."

Greeta couldn't help but take a quick glance across the room.

The woman at the opposite end had vanished.

CHAPTER 19

The next day Greeta and the men holding her captive trudged along a trail leading higher into the mountains, winding their way among pine trees growing straight and tall. She felt grateful for the shade. Without it, the steep climb would have made her too hot and sweaty.

By mid-day they reached a valley full of large animals bellowing mournfully.

"What are those?" Greeta said, staring at them.

"Cows," one of the men said. "He brought them over. They must be good climbers to get through the mountains. I've heard there's an easier path on the other side."

"Enough," Badger Face said, silencing

his companion with a menacing glance.

A stone wall stood waist-high between the edge of the valley and the forest. Greeta imagined its purpose was to keep the cows from wandering away and getting lost or killed by predators. She wedged her toes in spaces between the stones and climbed over the wall easily.

Many of the cows moved grudgingly while Greeta and the men walked around the edge of the valley. When a group of them blocked the way, Badger Face gave one a firm slap to make it move.

They followed the valley's curve, and Greeta saw a settlement up ahead. She noticed the sound of rushing water and assumed a river ran nearby. Making their way beyond the cattle, she saw a village similar to Oyster Bay, full of long wooden houses flanked by narrow rows of growing vegetables. Children chased each other, while their mothers sat around a communal fire, cutting vegetables and throwing them into a black pot hanging over the flames.

Iron.

She paused, staring at the pot. Even though iron was scarce, Greeta knew what it looked like. Papa had a knife he'd made himself many years ago in the Northlands.

How did these people find enough iron to make an entire pot?

And who had the skill to forge it?

Badger Face dug his fingers into Greeta's arm and dragged her with him. "Keep moving," he said.

Greeta shifted her attention ahead, and stared in wide-eyed wonder. The sound of rushing water came from a narrow waterfall pummeling down the cliff face now in front of her. A stone wall ran from where it contained the pool of water at the bottom of the waterfall to the far left where it channeled the water alongside the village and into the far side of the valley. Looking closer, she realized a structure had been built into the cliff by the waterfall. Greeta studied it, trying to wrap her mind around what she saw.

It looked like the cliff had been chiseled and shaped into a towering rock wall with windows carved into its surface. Carved steps lined the wall, leading from its base all the way up to the top with landings at different levels that led to open doorways. Stone steps had been laid from the wall's base down to the valley floor.

Greeta squinted, looking closer. Designs had also been carved into the rock wall, and she struggled to understand them. After a few moments, she realized it wasn't a series of varying designs. The towering rock wall standing next to the waterfall had been decorated with one enormous design. Based on everything Papa had told her, Greeta understood what now faced her.

The enormous rock wall bore the carving of a very detailed and elaborate dragon. The image twisted and turned across the stone surface, reminding Greeta of the beautiful silver brooch Auntie Peppa wore. The one created by Northlanders in the old days.

"I said keep moving!" Badger Face yanked her arm, dragging her with him.

Greeta hadn't realized it until now, but the sight of the carved dragon had stopped her in her tracks. She stumbled forward, trying to keep up with her captor's pace.

They approached the stone steps leading up to the base of the rock wall, and Greeta noticed a difference in the appearance of the people tending this area.

Women gathering water in pots from the pool. Men chiseling blocks from the raw cliff face to the far right of the dragon wall. Looking up at the sound of laughter, Greeta spotted a child running up the steps high above.

They all reminded her of Animosh. Greeta recognized characteristics of Northlander faces: a small nose and rounded cheekbones. But like the people of the Shining Star Nation, they each had a small stature along with dark hair and eyes. And while some had dark skin, others looked much paler.

How is this possible?

All of her life, Greeta believed she and her family were the only Northlanders who lived in the Great Turtle Lands. No traveler through her village had seen others like her. And no one who had travelled from her village, including Uncle Killing Crow, had ever encountered or heard of other Northlanders.

Following his companions, Badger Face led Greeta up the stone steps to a slim plateau where the dragon wall began. She then followed them up the stairs carved into the wall to the first open doorway.

Badger Face pulled her through it, and she found herself inside a cave. Greeta squinted, unable to see anything from the sudden change in light.

"We come with an offering," Badger Face said.

Her vision still adjusting, Greeta could only make out shadows bustling around them. As her vision grew used to the dim light behind the dragon wall, her surroundings astonished her. The cave had been carved with such precision that it looked as if it had been built out of massive blocks of stone, all of it streaked with black and gray. The stone floor beneath her feet felt perfectly level and smooth. She found herself in an enormous, high-ceilinged room with squared walls. Carved staircases leading to a balcony overlooking the room flanked each side. Gentle daylight streamed in from a row of tall and narrow windows carved near the ceiling, landing on the floor at the far side of the room.

Greeta glimpsed a few people scurrying up the stairs or through open doorways into the darkness, leaving her alone with her captors.

The sound of soft footsteps caught her attention, and she looked up to see a man bedecked in finery step through the light that had landed on the floor.

"Someone has brought an offering," he said, striding with the gait of a warrior on his way to the hunt.

Tall but slim, he dressed like no one Greeta had ever seen before, wearing bright blue breeches and a fine white shirt. Large silver brooches shaped like swirling dragons served to clasp a cloak at his neck, its bright blue material streaming behind him when he walked. Dozens of silver bracelets covered his arms, and rings crowded his fingers.

When he set his gaze on Greeta, he stopped short, his cloak swirling forward around his legs.

Greeta caught a glimpse of something long and narrow attached to his belt. She imagined it must be a sheathed sword, based on all the tales Papa had told her.

The man opened his mouth but seemed to be at a loss for words.

Greeta stared back, equaling the intensity she saw in his clear blue eyes. The man standing several paces in front of her looked to be older than Greeta but younger than Papa. The man's skin looked pale like hers, and his straight blond hair fell to his shoulders.

He's a Northlander. Just like me.

CHAPTER 20

Greeta stared at the cloaked man, too stunned to speak.

But he regained his senses quickly. Striding forward, he pointed at Greeta. "Who is she?" the man said in the language of the Shining Star Nation. "Where did you find her?"

"She came to us," Badger Face said. "She claims a shaman brought her, but we found no evidence of a shaman."

The man stopped directly in front of Greeta, keeping a steady gaze on her face. "She speaks Shining Star?"

The irritation Greeta always felt when people spoke about her as if she wasn't there trumped her intimidation. "Yes," she said in the language of her village, hearing the anger in her own voice, "she speaks Shining Star." A wave of rebellion surged through her. Switching languages, she said, "She also speaks Northlander."

The man standing before her looked as startled as if she'd slapped him. "Did you come here from the Northlands?"

"When I was a baby. I don't remember anything about it. I might not look it, but I'm a member of the Shining Star Nation."

"I remember the Northlands. I was cheated out of my inheritance when my uncle died." The man shook his head, his voice bitter and angry. "They gave me to brigands, who brought me here." He hesitated, seeming to change his mind about what to say. Smiling, he said, "And what of you and your shaman? How did you come to leave your village and end up here?"

Say as little as you can.

Startled, Greeta recognized the sound of Margreet's voice. She looked all around, expecting to see her.

But the only people she saw in the room were her captors and the Northlander man standing before her. Greeta didn't know if the words she'd heard were a memory from the Dreamtime or if Margreet's spirit had somehow followed and found a way to speak to her.

Maybe it didn't matter. Maybe all that mattered were the words themselves.

Greeta decided to heed Margreet's advice. "A shaman came to our village and offered to help us."

"She comes from a village of little consequence," Badger Face said.

"Which village?" the Northlander said, studying Greeta's face.

Keeping Margreet's words firmly in mind, Greeta said nothing.

Badger Face spoke up. "We think she comes from the Bay of Oysters."

Greeta focused on keeping her face neutral, determined not to let this Northlander man read her expression. Determined not to let him know that Badger Face had guessed correctly. If the Shining Star men who had brought her here were right, the Northlander might send them to her village and capture her family. Greeta could not let any harm come to them.

"The Bay of Oysters," the Northlander said. "That's south of the Blue Mountain."

Badger Face corrected him. "East. It's

part of the Crescent Valley by the coast."

The Northlander's gaze drifted to Greeta's neck. He reached toward it, and she instinctively took a step back.

He gripped her shoulder with one hand and held her steady while he picked up her necklace with the other. This close, he smelled like the morning after a cleansing rain storm, earthy and fresh. While he studied her pendant, the back of his hand rested warm against her skin. "This is a dragonfly. That's your name?" His breath smelled sweet, like fresh herbs.

Greeta saw no sense in denying it. "Yes."

While he fingered her pendant, studying it, his knuckles rubbed against the hollow between her breasts.

Greeta was surprised his touch didn't incense her. She didn't mind it. Instead, she found it pleasant.

"The body of the dragonfly. It's made of silver. It's shaped like a sword. Why?"

Still mindful to be wary of him, Greeta said, "My father always told me stories of swords and dragons."

"He made this." When the Northlander spoke, he made it sound like a statement, not a question. "Where did he get the silver? There's precious little of it here."

"He made it out of one of the rings he wore." Greeta noticed that like Papa, this man's fingers were covered with silver rings, and arm rings covered his sleeved biceps.

Nodding his understanding, the Northlander ran his thumb down the tiny sword. "Your father is a blacksmith."

Greeta swallowed hard, wondering if by some magical way he could see the secrets inside her. Fear seized her into silence.

The Northlander laughed. "I know your father is a blacksmith because I'm one myself. We work with iron. Anvils. Fire. Silversmithing is an entirely different skill. It requires the ability to work on a small scale, something most blacksmiths don't have." He placed the pendant back against Greeta's skin where it belonged, letting his hand linger. "I imagine your father made fine swords in his days, but this one is as rough and unfinished as anything I could make in silver."

Badger Face cleared his throat. "We could get to the Bay of Oysters in a few days. Bring anyone like her back here."

"No!" Greeta said, forgetting her fear. "Leave them alone."

A wry smile crossed the Northlander's face, and he turned toward the men who had brought Greeta to him. "No," he said. "Leave them alone."

Badger Face hesitated, a look of confusion crossing his face. "But you told us to be on the lookout. That's why we brought this one."

"This one is plenty for now," the Northlander said. "You can go home now. I will send word if I need more." He removed one of his silver arm rings and tossed it to Badger Face. "For a job well done."

Badger Face caught the arm ring with one hand and slid it on his own arm. His companions argued with him over how to divide the pay as they walked away.

Greeta felt anger growing inside her. Papa had taught her to choose happiness every morning and that most problems were small. She believed anger laid waste to happiness. But sometimes anger was the most appropriate response to a situation. When she spoke, she felt her anger rise like steam inside a covered pot. "Those men brought me here against my will. And you paid them to do that? What is wrong with you?"

The Northlander laughed. "I'm but a man longing to be among his own kind. Unless there are a great many like you back home, I dare say you sometimes feel the same."

Greeta's anger vanished, and she remembered the horrible morning she'd had a few days ago. She remembered her disappointment in Wapiti and the way her own cousin, Animosh, had betrayed and ridiculed her. She remembered the isolation that had overwhelmed her because her fellow villagers treated her like an outcast, even though she'd lived her entire life among them. She remembered the way she'd been taunted at Badger Face's village.

She looked at the Northlander, surprised by the new light in which she saw him. He might not have had the same experiences as Greeta, but he'd probably had very similar ones. He would know how she felt because he felt the same way.

She heard Margreet's voice again.

Don't forget how you got here.

"I do feel the same," Greeta said. "I want

to find out what it would be like to be among my own kind, more than just my Papa and Auntie." Her voice became more firm. "But I would never stoop to taking people against their will. How would you like it if someone did that to you?"

"That is precisely what happened to me."

Greeta stared at him, stunned. "What are you talking about? Isn't this your home? Aren't you the head of this community?"

The Northlander nodded. "That is my life now, but it was not always so." He looked away for a moment, and his eyes brimmed with tears when they met Greeta's again. "Everything that mattered was stripped away from me by evil people. They gave me to brigands, who forced me to be their servant while they traveled from place to place, pillaging and killing anyone who got in their way."

Greeta listened with caution, not sure what to think of his story. "This happened in the Northlands?"

"It began in the Northlands. Then they joined forces with others and followed a leader named Krystr. We sailed on ships throughout the Northlands and then the Midlands and Southlands. Eventually, we joined his camp. I'd never seen anything like it. So many soldiers. So many tents, all of them colored blue and filling up an entire valley. Enough to make you feel like a fish in the sea. And the leader's tent with its pole standing high above all the others and covered with ribbons flying in the wind. At night there were so many lights inside his tent it glowed like the moon." He paused and sighed. "But I'd never agreed to be one of them. The brigands who owned me never allowed me to be more than their servant. I didn't want to be there."

Greeta studied his face as if it were a lengthy trail she needed to follow, looking everywhere for anything that might pose a threat to her safety. "How did you end up here?"

The Northlander took a deep breath, seeming to steady himself. "I found a few others like myself. Mostly boys impatient to become men. One night a commotion happened in the tent of the leader, Krystr. A lot of shouting. And men seemed to be chasing someone from his tent out among the others. Some tents caught fire. I knew that kind of chaos was like a gift I might never know again, so I ran through the camp and gathered up the boys who wanted to get out. A river ran close to camp, and that's where the ships were kept."

Greeta frowned, wondering if he lied and decided to challenge his words. "Ships on a river? How is that possible? Do you mean they had canoes? Or small boats?"

"No. Northlander ships can navigate rivers or oceans equally well. They're long but have shallow depth and perfect balance. Using oars makes it possible to steer through rivers, and putting up the sail gives the ship the power to skim through ocean waves. It's how Krystr and his army conquered the lands: they could travel anywhere easily and arrive without warning." He crossed his arms. "The guards at the river were confused by the shouting and the fires in the camp. Some of them ran toward it. In the cover of chaos and darkness, we stole aboard one of the empty ships and slipped away before anyone realized a ship had gone missing. There were dozens of them. The guards probably didn't know they'd lost one until the next morning."

"And after you stole the ship?"

The Northlander grinned. "One of the boys who came with me had heard tales of this country. A few of the men he'd served had sailed here and relived those days by talking about them. The boy had paid attention whenever the men talked and committed what he learned to memory. None of us wanted to fight or put ourselves in danger by serving soldiers, so we decided to start a new life. One we could call our own. We crossed the great ocean and landed here many years ago."

Greeta mulled over his story. When Badger Face and his men first led her into this settlement, she'd seen many people of the Shining Star Nation and several half-bloods like Animosh. But this man was the only one who looked like her. "The boys who came with you. They must be men by now. Where are they?"

A strain of sadness darkened his face. "When we first landed, we discovered a river leading inland from the sea. We followed it here, but the climb is treacherous. I alone survived."

When she spoke, Greeta noticed the

disbelief in her voice. "You sailed a ship here? Into the mountains?"

The Northlander smirked. "I can show you. But I've forgotten my manners." He gave her a quick bow. "My name is Fine-hurst." Pointing at her pendant, he said, "And I take it your name is Dragonfly."

For the first time in her life, Greeta didn't envy people who had only one name. She didn't want this man to know she'd been named after Margreet. She didn't want him to know her family called her Greeta. For now, her Shining Star name might be enough to protect the people she loved from him. "Yes," Greeta said. "They call me Dragonfly."

CHAPTER 21

Greeta walked by Finehurst's side while he led her through the cave-like maze that appeared to be his home. Beams of light filtering through the cave from windows carved high above made its smooth stone surfaces look golden. The air felt cool and clean.

"Once I climbed up the mountain," he said, "I had to traverse my way around it. That done, I came across a tribe of Shining Star people living in the valley. Of course, back then I didn't know their language, and I tried to act out what had happened. How we'd sailed the ship until there was nowhere else to go and then how all my friends had fallen off the mountain to their deaths."

Greeta kept hoping to hear Margreet's voice again, but it had gone silent. She didn't find Finehurst's story convincing. "You must be an awfully good climber to accomplish what none of your friends could do."

Finehurst's chest puffed out in pride. "I dare say I am. Of course, I come from an especially mountainous part of the Northlands, while my friends hailed from the Midlands and the Southlands, which tend to be flatter. Their experience paled compared to mine." He went quiet for a moment and then added what sounded like an afterthought meant for Greeta's benefit. "Poor fellows."

Greeta noted everything she saw: small rooms filled with clay pots of harvested grain and seeds, open areas and staircases leading up to higher levels, narrow passageways leading deeper into the cave.

"Curious?"

Greeta turned to see Finehurst watching her intently. She hurried to cover her own intent to gather information that could help her escape and find her way back home. Offering the warmest smile she could muster, Greeta said, "Everything is so beautiful. I didn't know the Shining Star people could create something like this."

"That's because they can't," Finehurst said. "Not without my teachings."

Not convinced of his boast, Greeta decided to stay quiet. She believed she'd learn more by letting him talk than by confronting him. "Northlander teachings?"

Finehurst nodded, gesturing for her to walk ahead of him when they reached a passageway too narrow for them to walk side by side. "When I first traveled with the brigands, we went to the far north where they took control of a small village and forced them to dig through a mountain because they'd heard legends of its heart being made of silver."

Greeta turned her head to look back at him, wanting to see his expression. "Was it?"

Finehurst shrugged. "We found a bit. Not much. But the brigands wanted to live in comfort while this happened, so they made some of the villagers carve out places to live inside the mountain. The brigands made me work with the villagers, and I learned how to do this sort of thing."

Wanting to pump up his pride and make him at ease about revealing more information, Greeta said, "Everything here is so beautiful."

"It would be even finer if I'd had the time to do the work myself, but I had other things that needed my attention."

Greeta stopped abruptly when the passageway split in two. "Which way?"

Sliding past her, Finehurst took her by the hand and led her into the left branch of the passageway. "Prepare yourself to see something quite splendid."

The light ahead grew stronger, and a short time later they emerged outside onto a wide ledge. Greeta gaped at mountains towering all around, forming a circle around a deep chasm filled with a lake. The cliffs surrounding the water were so sheer that she now believed all of Finehurst's companions actually might have died trying to scale them. A fine mist hovered around them, clinging to the mountainsides, and white clouds dotted the bright sky above. Below, a hawk screeched, circling above the lake.

"It is the source of the river we followed from the sea," Finehurst said, pointing at the lake. "But you have yet to see the best. Follow me."

Well aware that if she fell from the ledge, the long fall toward the lake would end in certain death, Greeta clung to the side of the mountain while Finehurst walked without a care along the edge. Several moments later he stopped, pointing down at the water. "There!"

Greeta strained, unable to see anything out of the ordinary.

Finehurst looked around for her, noticing how far she held back. "You can't see it from there. Come closer."

Still nervous, Greeta let go of the mountainside and spread her arms out to balance herself, even though the ledge stood wide and solid beneath her feet. She inched her way toward Finehurst. But when she caught sight of what Finehurst pointed out, her fear fell away and she walked near the edge to get a better look.

"It's a ship," Greeta said, recognizing it at once even though the only one she'd ever seen had been much farther away. "A Northlander ship." She looked up at Finehurst. "Then it was you I saw several days ago. You had this ship at sea."

Finehurst took a sharp breath in, staring at her. "When? Exactly when?"

"A few days before those men brought me here. Five days ago, I think."

"You saw a ship like mine? A Northlander ship?"

Looking back at Finehurst's ship, Greeta took in every detail of it that she could make out from this distance. "Of course. Papa told me about them all the time I was growing up. I know what they look like. It's just that yours was the first one I'd ever seen."

Finehurst took her by the shoulders, turning her to face him squarely. "The last time my ship sailed was a month ago. The ship you saw couldn't have been mine." His eyes narrowed. "Tell me where you were when you saw that ship."

CHAPTER 22

With his hands still on her shoulders, Finehurst turned them both until he stood between Greeta and the rising wall so that she stood only steps away from the cliff's edge behind her back. "Tell me where you saw the ship like mine."

Unwilling to give him any information that would lead Finehurst to her village, Greeta struggled to think of a story he'd believe. "I saw it before those men took me."

Finehurst considered her for a long moment, staring into her eyes. "I know those men and their people. They said you came to them, which means you arrived in their village. They live nowhere near the sea."

Thinking quickly, Greeta lied. "But I traveled along the shore many days before I found their village. I saw the ship at sea when I walked south."

"South," Finehurst said, rolling the word around in his mouth like a firm, round berry. "That means you came from the north. There is only one good way from their village to the north shore, and that would place you near the Mistful Bay." He paused, smiling while keeping a firm grip on her shoulders. "Tell me, what did you think of that landscape?"

He's testing me. He wants to find out if I was where I said I was.

Although Greeta had never traveled outside of her village until now, she remembered the tales Uncle Killing Crow had told for years about his travels with other men from their village to hunt and trade with other tribes in the Shining Star Nation. She remembered one particular story he told about Mistful Bay.

"I like the rocky shore," Greeta said, returning Finehurst's steady gaze. "It's slippery to walk along the shore, but I found a spot where I could wade into the water." Remembering the details of Uncle

Killing Crow's story, she said, "I found the best clams I've ever tasted. But the bay isn't well named. The locals say it sometimes fills with mist, but not as often you'd think when you hear its name. I happened to be there on an especially clear day." Shifting back to what she'd seen days ago in her own village, Greeta said, "After that I happened to look out to the horizon, and that's when I saw the ship. Far away on the edge of the horizon."

"Why did you think it was mine?"

"I saw the outline of it. The way the body of the ship sits low and long in the water. I saw the shape of a dragon's head at one end. And its sail stood large and square, just like everything my papa ever told me about every Northlander ship he's ever seen. Just like the one that brought us from the Northlands to the Great Turtle Lands."

Finehurst stepped forward, forcing Greeta to step back. "Why do I have a difficult time believing you?"

Fear caught in her throat when she felt the edge of the cliff with her heel. But then Margreet's voice whispered in her ear.

You are not helpless! Remember how I

have trained you.

Greeta had been to the Dreamtime only a few times, but the last time it seemed like she'd been there for days while Margreet trained her in sword work. But she had no weapons to use. No way to defend herself. All she had was her hands.

An idea came to Greeta. She grabbed onto each side of Finehurst's cloak, and then wrapped each fist in the cloth, anchoring herself to the man who threatened her. "If you push me, I'll take you with me," she said.

Surprise registered on Finehurst's face, and he went still. When he released his hands from Greeta's shoulders, she kept her fists wrapped tightly in the cloak. She smiled at the dragon-shaped silver pin attaching the cloak to his shirt at the throat.

Laughing, Finehurst slipped his hands around her waist, lifting Greeta and spinning until they both landed a safe distance from the cliff's edge. Placing her on the ground, Finehurst kept his hands on her waist. "You're a feisty one."

Before Greeta could answer, his lips pressed against hers.

Stunned, she pushed him away. "What are you doing?" She backed away until the stone wall behind her stopped her progress.

Flanking her with his hands against the wall, Finehurst faced her. "Doesn't it occur to you that the gods of our people might have brought you here? That they might deem we should be together for the sake of our people?" He gazed down at her body. "Hasn't it crossed your mind that we could make beautiful babies? Children with flaxen hair and eyes like the sea?"

Greeta tried to duck under his arm, but Finehurst caught her, taking her hands and pinning them above her head against the wall. "You talk about our people, but you forget how a Northlander is expected to treat a woman."

Finehurst licked his lips. "I have done nothing inappropriate. I have not harmed you. And there is no law against stealing a kiss."

"There should be!" Greeta wriggled, unable to break free. "My papa has warned me about scoundrels like you!"

His touch softened. Releasing Greeta's hands, he slipped his fingers into her hair, caressing her jaw line with his thumbs. "Forgive me," Finehurst said, his voice soft and full of longing. "It's been such a long time since I've seen a real Northlander woman with true Northlander spirit. It does my heart good. Looking at you feeds my starving soul."

Greeta knew she should push him away, but no one had ever touched her like this before, not even Wapiti in the days when they flirted with the idea of becoming lovers, something that had never come to fruition. She wanted to ignore the way Finehurst looked into her eyes, but instead she remembered how the young men in her village shirked her.

"Such beauty," Finehurst murmured, stroking her hair. He stood strong and tall above her, unlike most men of the Shining Star Nation who stood only as tall as Greeta's shoulders. Except, of course, for Wapiti, who stood eye to eye with her.

She remembered how easily Wapiti had believed Animosh's lies about Greeta. The least he could have done was stand up for her as a friend. Instead, he had mooned over a married woman who should have been taking care of her children.

Finehurst rested his forehead against hers and whispered, "I thought I'd never find a woman like you. I'd given up. Please tell me I don't have to give up again."

She thought about how she'd felt like an outcast when she left her village with Shadow, the shaman who abandoned her. Greeta remembered how the people in Badger Face's village had ridiculed her. Only Papa and Auntie Peppa and Uncle Killing Crow cared about her.

Even though it hurt, Greeta forced herself to remember the truth she'd realized when Auntie Peppa had told her goodbye. No matter how many years she and Wapiti had been friends, no matter how much she thought he cared about her, it had all been for nothing. No Shining Star man would ever want her. She could never have a family of her own with any man native to the Great Turtle Lands.

And the worst truth was that the people of her village had made it clear she didn't belong. It wasn't her home anymore, and she had to find a new one.

She felt the tension drain from her body, softening under Finehurst's touch.

What if this place could be her new

home? What if she could be accepted here? What if she could fit in?

Finehurst tilted his head, finding her lips once more with his.

When Greeta felt the warmth of his tongue press against the line where her lips met, she opened them, letting him inside to kiss her fully and completely. She sensed his longing, but his slow and gentle kiss awakened her own sense of longing, something she'd once felt for Wapiti. Finehurst's simple but thorough kiss suddenly felt like an act much more intimate.

Shuddering with pleasure, Greeta squirmed away from him.

Looking at the empty hands that had been caressing her hair moments ago, Finehurst said, "Did I do something to displease you?"

"No," Greeta said. "But there are proper and improper ways for a Northlander man to show his feelings for a Northlander woman who is not already his wife." Realizing she still trembled with pleasure, she crossed her arms, trying to both compose herself and present a stern front.

"Of course there are." Finehurst mi-

micked her, crossing his own arms. "Is that what you want? To become my wife before we get carried away with ourselves?"

The way he looked at her made Greeta nervous. Finehurst made no attempt to hide his desire for her. "No! Not right now, at least. Not at this very moment."

"What do you want?"

Greeta cleared her throat, still fighting nerves. This strange turn of events was the last thing she would have expected when Badger Face and his companions brought her to Finehurst. "We should take time to get to know each other. To find out if we'd be compatible."

"There are many ways of being compatible. We should explore them all." Finehurst smirked.

"Fine," Greeta said. "But we'll do it my way and in my time, just like all Northlander women do."

Finehurst bowed. "As you command, young mistress. Give me your bidding, for I am your slave."

CHAPTER 23

Greeta allowed Finehurst to take her hand and lead her back into his mansion carved into the mountain. She followed him up a stairway that spiraled upward like the shell of a snail and led into a small room dominated by what appeared to be a bed: a large pallet of straw covered with the furs of black bears. Square windows lined one wall, and Greeta walked to them and looked outside to find a spectacular view of the lake and Finehurst's ship far below. "So beautiful."

"Then you are certain to like this," Finehurst said, joining her side. "Notice the wooden panel above each window."

Looking up, Greeta saw the detail of swirling and twisting Northlander designs of animals on the panels.

"Each panel has been fit into a track carved into the stone so that you can close each window properly." Finehurst slid the panel until it covered the window directly in front of Greeta, not only blocking out the light but creating a seal preventing drafts. "You will stay cool in the summer and warm in the winter."

Greeta ran her hand across the design carved into the wood. She recognized the thin, stick-like figure of a horse and admired how its legs and tail extended into curling lines that formed a delicate pattern around it. It reminded her of the brooches Auntie Peppa wore.

"Likewise, you can make your own fires here," Finehurst said, gesturing to a hearth-like area built into the same wall. "You are most likely used to having fires in the center of your home with a hole in the roof for the smoke to escape. Perhaps you will appreciate what we have done here. The hearth is large enough for a good fire, but there is a space carved above it inside the wall that then exits out the same wall. The smoke can escape, but any air coming into this room is warmed by the fire."

Greeta nodded and turned to examine the rest of the room. Behind the bed an enormous tapestry covered the wall, filled with images of men fighting dragons and other creatures.

"This is the favorite of all my possessions," Finehurst said, striding over to the tapestry and laying a gentle hand on it. "I happened upon it in my travels, and it survived the crossing of the sea especially well."

Still suspicious of his stories, Greeta kept her voice soft when she spoke because she didn't want him to realize she was challenging him. "You happened upon it? How did that come about?"

Finehurst beamed at her. "I was in the Southlands and came across a fine mansion where the master lived with his wife and many children, almost all of them boys. I'd come with many men, and we helped the family. Their gratitude for us was so great that they made this a gift to us. It tells their family history."

Greeta reminded herself that Finehurst had told her he'd been given to brigands and traveled with them until he could break free. She suspected the truth behind this story was that the brigands had stolen the tapestry and probably everything else they thought had some value. "And how did you happen to be the one who ended up with it?"

"I was the only one who wanted it."

Although nodding her understanding, Greeta doubted that part of his story as well. The tapestry looked like something that had been passed down for many generations and probably had great value. She'd never met a brigand, but Papa and Auntie Peppa had told her stories about them. How they roamed the Northlands. How they robbed people traveling the roads and pillaged villages. More than likely, Finehurst had found a way to weasel the tapestry away from the brigands who'd possessed him.

Looking back at Finehurst, she said, "And what is the purpose of this room?"

"Didn't I make that clear?" He laughed, seeming to share a joke with himself. "This is your room."

"Mine?"

"Yours and yours alone."

Greeta shifted her weight from one foot to the other, uncertain how she felt. "Are you holding me prisoner?"

Finehurst walked to one of the open windows and gazed outside. "No. I'm inviting you to be my guest for as long as you wish. And if you find a place in your heart for me, I will ask you to be my wife."

Greeta sank onto the edge of the bed, running her hands through the black fur piled on top of it. This was a room where she could sleep warm and well. "And what if I said I want to go home now? That I don't want to wait here another minute?"

Heaving a sigh that carried the weight of the world, Finehurst kept looking out the window. When he finally spoke, his voice broke as if he had to struggle to keep from weeping. "I would feel the greatest distress I have ever known, but I would honor your wishes because I want you to be happy. My men are at your disposal, and I would insist that they escort you safely to your father's side."

More confused than ever, Greeta let her hands rest against the soft fur. Finehurst spoke as if he genuinely cared for her, even though they'd just met. That seemed impossible. Greeta's feelings for Wapiti had begun with a childhood friendship and grown slowly over the years into love.

And look how that ended up. With Wapiti mooning over my own cousin and ridiculing me behind my back. Did Wapiti's feelings for me really change that much? Did he ever love me? Did I only see what I wanted to see?

Greeta shrugged off her thoughts, not sure what to believe about Wapiti. "And if I decide to stay for a few days and then ask to return home?"

Finehurst spoke so softly that Greeta could barely hear him. "Those few days would be the happiest of my life. And the day you leave will be the worst." He took a deep breath as if gathering courage. "But I only want what's best for you. And if the only way you can be happy is in the village you know, then there you must go."

Mulling over his words, Greeta decided she had little to lose. What harm would it do to spend a few days here? After all, she felt more welcome by Finehurst than she did in her own village. Papa had sent her off with the shaman, so he wouldn't be worried about her. The shaman hadn't told them when to expect Greeta to return or even if she'd return at all. And why did the shaman disappear? Greeta resisted the urge to snort in disgust at the way she'd been treated with such disregard by the shaman, not wanting Finehurst to think he'd done anything wrong. It seemed like he was the only one who wanted and valued her company.

"All right. I'll stay for awhile."

Beaming, Finehurst faced her. Taking large strides toward her, he picked Greeta up in his arms and spun her around. "I'm the happiest man alive!"

When he set her back down so her feet touched the floor, Greeta felt dizzy, as if the world now spun around her. "Perhaps," she said, "I'm the luckiest woman."

Taking her by the hand, Finehurst said, "Let me prove it to you. Come see how much I have to offer."

CHAPTER 24

Greeta followed Finehurst while he took her to every room inside his mansion carved into the mountainside. Although the rooms for storing food and pottery had roughly hewn floors and walls, every other space had a polished and smooth appearance. Light streamed from high windows carved into all sides of the mountain. People of the Shining Star Nation bustled in and out, stepping aside to let Finehurst and Greeta pass when they met in narrow hallways.

"Do they work for you?" Greeta said.

"In a manner of speaking. They had already claimed this mountain as their home when my men and I arrived."

The men who died trying to climb up the

mountain from the lake.

Finehurst gestured toward everything surrounding him. "In mild weather, the Shining Star people prefer to live outside. But in the winter, they move into the rooms on the lowest level. It is a far more pleasant way to live than what they'd known before my arrival, and they show their gratitude by deferring to me."

Pausing in the center of a long hallway flanked by tall doorways, Greeta noticed a lighter-skinned woman pass across one of them. The woman reminded her of cousin Animosh, daughter of Auntie Peppa and Uncle Killing Crow.

If none of Finehurst's men survived, that means only one man could be that woman's father. And she's not the first one I've seen today.

Not wanting to reveal anything about her own family, Greeta chose her words carefully. "I notice some of the Shining Star people don't look like the others. They don't look full blooded."

"Ah, yes," Finehurst said. For the first time, a sheepish look crossed his face, reminding Greeta of a young boy caught doing something wrong. "How do I explain?"

Greeta cleared her throat. "I think it's obvious. There are no other Northlanders here, and the people I've seen appear to have some Northlander qualities." She looked directly into his eyes, standing firm and facing him squarely, ready to do whatever necessary to make it clear she expected to hear the truth. "You are the only one who could father such children."

Expecting his face to color in shame, Greeta was surprised when Finehurst held his head up high and returned her direct gaze.

"You tell the truth," he said. "When I first arrived, when all my friends and colleagues who had sailed across the sea by my side perished, I felt alone. I felt lost."

Tears welled in Finehurst's eyes, startling Greeta. Up until this moment his manner had struck her as proud and somewhat brash, like a warrior. It hadn't occurred to her that he could show such sensitivity as well. She felt the door to her heart open ever so slightly, realizing for the first time that since Wapiti had betrayed her love, she'd placed a wall around her heart without realizing it.

Be careful, a voice inside her said. A voice that sounded a bit like Margreet. *He may not be the man he pretends to be.*

Greeta hesitated, taking the point and keeping it in mind. "So you took a wife? Where is she? I'd like to meet her."

Finehurst surprised her by laughing. "I took no wife. I have never married." His gaze intensified. "I've never met a woman I would want to have in my marriage bed until today."

An image of Finehurst's bed ran through Greeta's mind, making her feel embarrassed and vulnerable. Even worse, she imagined his touch upon her naked skin. Flustered, Greeta said, "You have no wife and yet you have several children?"

Gesturing for her to follow while Finehurst led the way to a large, open room, he said, "When I arrived, this particular tribe of the Shining Star Nation had a problem. A band of men from the Red Rock nation had come here in search of new land. New food. New shelter. The Shining Star people turned this spot into a fortress and fought back when the Red Rock tribe attacked, ultimately sending them away. But the Red Rock battle left many Shining

Star men dead and dying. Most of those men were young husbands who had yet to father many children, if any at all. Their widows wanted to be comforted and long-ed to have children."

A lump formed in Greeta's throat. She knew that longing all too well. The sting of losing her dream to have children and spend her life with Wapiti still throbbed painfully in her belly.

Finehurst shrugged. "I was the best solution. If any Shining Star man had comforted the widows, he would have risked his own marriage. Would you want your husband to father another woman's child?"

"No." Greeta answered so softly she could barely hear her own voice. She remembered the way Wapiti looked at Ani-mosh, her cousin and a married woman at that. "It would break my heart."

"But I had no wife. No one to hurt." He sighed. "And truth be told, I needed comfort, too. I'd just sailed across the great ocean, which took many days. I'd just lost all my companions from the Northlands. I felt lonely, just like the widows. We took comfort in each other's arms. They made me feel welcome. They made me feel that I'd found a new home. They made me feel like I could begin a new life here." Finehurst let his gaze linger on Greeta's body, seeming to examine it and find pleasure at the sight. "And I made them feel good."

A twinge of jealousy sparked inside Greeta. "Do you still make them feel good?"

Finehurst smirked. "From time to time." He reached one hand toward Greeta's face and smoothed her hair back with a light touch. "But I've always longed for a Northlander girl, and I would give up my dalliances in a heartbeat for the right girl." He stepped close enough to whisper in her ear. "I would touch only the woman I love. I would bring her and her alone to ecstasy inside my arms. All of my future children would be hers and hers alone."

Be careful. What if he's telling you these things only because he believes you want to hear them?

Finehurst nuzzled his nose against Greeta's ear. "I would be her slave, especially when I took her to bed. I would do everything she asked of me. Without hesitation. I would live to please her."

Greeta closed her eyes and leaned forward, resting her forehead against Finehurst's shoulder. She wished Wapiti had said such words to her. She'd dreamed of him saying such things. All these years, she'd assumed Wapiti wanted her in the same way she wanted him.

And now someone else wanted her instead. A Northlander, like Greeta. A strong and powerful man, desired by many women. A man willing to give her shelter inside the most beautiful place she'd ever seen.

For the first time, her lifelong love and longing for Wapiti began to fade. What if it had existed only for the purpose of leading her here to Finehurst? What if the shaman Shadow's true mission had been to lead Greeta to a place where she was bound to end up at Finehurst's doorstep?

Greeta didn't know what to believe. Papa and Auntie Peppa had told her stories about the Northlander gods and goddesses, the spirits of earth and wind and fire and water, who sometimes came to mortals and spoke to them. On the other hand, Uncle Killing Crow and other people of the Shining Star Nation had told her stories about one Great Spirit and other lesser spirits, who had powerful light in their veins, like the moon and the stars in the sky. Such spirits sometimes led people on paths of destiny. Were Papa and Auntie Peppa right when they spoke of Northlander beliefs? Or could there really be spirits in the Great Turtle Lands who helped mortals reach their destiny?

Or could both exist? Could there still be gods and goddesses in the Northlands as well as great spirits in the Great Turtle Lands? Did powerful beings live in different parts of the world? Or could the Northlander gods and the spirits of the Great Turtle Lands be one and the same?

Finehurst let his hand sink into her hair, pulling gently to raise her face to meet his own. "Would you like that? Would you like me to please you in every way you wish?"

"I think so," Greeta whispered, her emotions teetering on a cliff, tempted to fall into the conviction that Finehurst must be the man deemed by the spirits as her intended.

Cradling her head with his hand,

Finehurst leaned forward and kissed her with a deeper and more passionate intent.

But then the room shook with the reverberation of a blood-curdling scream.

CHAPTER 25

Finehurst pushed Greeta away and shouted, "Stay here!"

The sudden change in his demeanor startled her. Moments ago he'd been tender and loving. Now he looked like an animal that had been caged against its will, wild and eager to wreak havoc against those who had put it behind bars.

Ripping his cloak off and casting it aside, Finehurst pulled a polished sword from the scabbard at his waist, a sword whose length almost matched Greeta's height. Balancing the flat of the blade on his shoulder, Finehurst dashed away, heading toward the entrance of his carved-rock mansion.

Greeta followed, running down a hallway. All around her, men and women of the Shining Star Nation ran through the rooms and passageways, their shouts echoing. Several men raced past her, and Greeta started when someone took her hand. Looking back, she saw a light-skinned woman who looked to be Greeta's age, and she immediately thought of Animosh, bristling at the woman's touch.

"Come this way!" the woman said.

Greeta stood her ground, not knowing what to do. "Why? What's happening?"

"The dragon," the woman holding her hand said. "It's broken free again!"

Dragon?

"There are no dragons here," Greeta said. "They lived in the Northlands, but they were dying out. They don't exist anymore."

The light-skinned woman let go of Greeta's hand. "If you don't hide with us, it could break in here and kill you!"

Greeta shook her head in disbelief. What could this woman possibly be talking about? A bear, perhaps?

Giving up, the light-skinned woman ran back into the depths of Finehurst's mansion.

Greeta guessed she stood in a room located at least one story above ground. Looking up, she saw light streaming from the direction in which Finehurst had run. A window had to be nearby. That meant she could look outside to find out what kind of creature the light-skinned woman claimed to be a dragon while staying safe at the same time. She hurried through a few passageways until she found a window facing the courtyard she'd walked through earlier today.

The window had a smooth and polished sill, possibly from the touch of many people leaning on it throughout the years since it had been carved. It felt cool when Greeta placed both hands on it and peered outside.

Below in the courtyard, an animal unlike anything Greeta had ever seen made her heart race. Looking like a giant lizard, she figured its length must be about the same as one horse standing behind another. Its dark scales glistened in the sunlight, and its long tail whipped from side to side. Even from this distance, she could see the creature's long, curved claws dig into the earth and noticed scraping marks it had already created.

In a world of confusion, Greeta froze, staring at the animal. She thought she had seen every animal that lived in the Great Turtle Lands, either alive or when a hunting party brought home its success. Greeta knew all manner of small animals ranging from fox to beaver. She knew deer and bear and bison.

But staring at an animal she'd never laid eyes on before terrified her and made her feel as if the world she knew had been keeping secrets from her.

Important secrets that she needed to learn and understand.

"It *is* a dragon," she whispered, remembering everything Papa and Auntie Peppa had told her about them.

And then she realized only one man stood in the courtyard, facing the dragon.

Finehurst.

An overwhelming sense of panic for his safety made Greeta forget the misgivings she'd felt just minutes ago. She thought she heard Margreet's voice begin to whisper in her ear, but Finehurst's shouts drowned out any other sound.

"Come on, you slimy beast!" Finehurst

yelled. He held onto his sword with both hands, pointing its tip directly at the dragon's open jaw, teeming with jagged teeth. He stood alone in the courtyard with it, although Greeta noticed some Shining Star people huddled behind rocks and walls nearby.

Greeta shuddered, steadying her elbows on the windowsill and covering her eyes with her hands, wanting to turn away but unable to will herself to do so. She couldn't bear to see Finehurst injured, but she needed to see the dragon. She opened her fingers and peeked through them.

Finehurst circled the animal, keeping a steady grip on the sword. The dragon kept an equally steady eye on the man, turning in place to watch him. Its fat belly hung low, dragging in the dirt. Spittle hung in strings from its jaw. Its eyes glinted in the sunlight, and Greeta believed she saw intelligence in them. That intelligence made her feel conflicted.

Growing up in the Shining Star Nation, Greeta had learned to respect all animals as brothers and sisters. When a hunting party returned with deer or elk or moose, all people thanked the animal's spirit for its sacrifice so that they could live by eating its body. Uncle Killing Crow told stories about meeting bears, bowing to them in honor, and continuing on his way, unharmed because the bears returned his respect. But every so often bears wayward in their nature, whether diseased in body or spirit, would attack men and kill them.

Just as this dragon seemed to be on the verge of doing to Finehurst.

"Ha!" Finehurst yelled in the courtyard below. He waved the sword over his head with both hands and then pointed its tip at the animal and lunged toward it.

The beast moved lightning quick, darting out of the sword's path and nipping at Finehurst before backing away. The dragon's tail whipped back and forth, like a cat toying with a mouse.

Greeta's throat tightened. The Shining Star people had taught her to respect animals and to be aware of their nature. But Papa had told her stories of dragons in the Northlands, creatures with bites so deadly that their prey were poisoned to death within days or even hours. Violent creatures that ravaged crops and villages, leaving dozens to hundreds to thousands of people dead and their food destroyed.

That's why dragons always had to be killed. Papa said if the Shining Star people ever saw a dragon, they'd understand and would not hesitate to destroy it.

Finehurst's missed blow had carried him to the center of the courtyard. The dragon now circled him, dragging the back of each paw forward against the ground and then plopping it upright to take a step. Its long yellow tongue flicked rapidly.

When Finehurst shifted his grip and raised the sword above his head to prepare for an overhead blow, the dragon charged at him. The beast butted its head against Finehurst's belly so hard that Greeta heard the air knocked out of the man's lungs. Knocked off his feet, Finehurst flew backwards through the air, landing hard on his back.

The sword lay nearby, knocked out of his hands.

"No," Greeta whispered, terrified.

The dragon slapped a paw on Finehurst's chest, pinning him to the ground. It sniffed at his face.

Finehurst whimpered, closing his eyes while one frantic hand reached uselessly toward his sword, just out of reach.

Anger stirred inside Greeta, unlike any kind of anger she'd felt before. It began with the memory of how she'd loved Wapiti her entire life only to watch him betray her because he'd become smitten with her married cousin. The way Badger Face and his men had treated her and made her believe her family could be hurt kindled that anger. And now, just when it looked like she might have found the true love of her life, the man who could father the children she longed to have, an animal threatened to kill him.

All of it sparked a flame that burned throughout Greeta's entire body, making her forget her fear. Leaning out the window, she called out. "Leave him be!"

Keeping a firm paw on Finehurst, the dragon followed her voice, looking up at her. Eyes sparkling in the sunlight, it studied her for several long moments.

Greeta's voice rang true and loud. She forgot any misgivings she'd had about Finehurst just minutes ago. "He is mine!"

The dragon looked down at Finehurst and then back up at Greeta, seemingly surprised.

Do dragons understand mortal speech?

Not knowing the answer, Greeta decided to keep talking. Maybe it understood words. Or maybe it understood intent. "You have no right to be here! Get out!"

The dragon hissed. Agitated, it swatted Finehurst away with one paw and then paced below Greeta's window.

Finehurst rolled in the dirt like a rag doll, finally coming to rest far behind the dragon near the edge of the courtyard. Shaking, Finehurst curled up on his side and moaned.

Greeta kept her focus on the dragon, now feeling angry that Finehurst wasn't already attacking it again. She knew if she gave in to the luxury of looking at Finehurst directly, the beast would most likely follow her gaze and close in for the kill. For some reason she couldn't fathom, she had the dragon's attention and meant to keep it in order to give Finehurst a chance to run away or fight again.

"Why do you come here?" Greeta shouted. "To kill us? To eat us?"

The dragon whipped its head back and forth, stomping its paw against the ground.

Is the dragon telling me no? Then why would it come here?

Or am I just imagining things?

Finehurst remained curled up on the ground. Was he injured? Greeta kept her eyes on the dragon but hoped her words would inspire Finehurst to do something. "Don't make me come down there, because I will pick up that sword and use it."

The dragon paused and looked as if it might be smiling.

Greeta cast more accusations at the dragon below. "If you didn't come to kill us, then you came to kill our cattle. You came to steal our food! Thief!"

The dragon stared directly into her eyes for several long moments and then snorted, as if in disgust.

The stories Uncle Killing Crow told about showing honor to bears crossed her mind again. Could it be possible that showing respect to a dragon might work?

Finehurst stirred and righted himself. He scanned the courtyard until he spotted his sword.

Greeta let her anger fade away. More interested in trying to understand the dragon than in Finehurst, she studied the beast. Her voice remained loud, but now she called down as if she were talking to a family member. "I don't understand. You're not here to kill us or steal our food. Then why are you here?"

The dragon paced from side to side for a few moments. It halted and looked up at her.

Finehurst attacked the animal from behind, slashing his sword against its body, but his blows glanced off the protective scales.

Startled, the dragon whipped its head around to stare at Finehurst. When it charged once more with its head down, Finehurst tossed the sword aside, scrambled to the edge of the courtyard, and picked up a small boulder, which he immediately brought down on the beast's head.

Dazed, the dragon collapsed.

Finehurst snapped his fingers, and dozens of Shining Star people streamed from the sidelines carrying rope. Before the creature had time to recover, they had its jaw closed shut and it paws bound so that it could take only the smallest steps.

Surprised, Greeta realized she didn't

want them to hurt the dragon. She bolted, racing through the maze of Finehurst's mountain mansion until she found her way outside to the courtyard. She arrived in time to see Finehurst brushing the dirt from his clothing and the Shining Star people nudging the bound dragon through a doorway on the far side of the mansion.

She ran to Finehurst's side. "I need to see the dragon."

Finehurst laughed. "I'd think you'd rather see me." When he looked at her, the expression in his eyes was dark and disappointed. "I'd think you'd say are you all right, my darling? Did the awful beast harm you?"

"Of course, but I can see you're all right." Greeta studied him in the same way she'd studied the dragon. She chose her words carefully. "But it's the first time I've ever seen a beast like that. I've heard about them all my life, but I never dreamed I'd ever have the chance to see one."

Finehurst ignored her, returning his attention to brushing the courtyard dirt from his clothing.

Greeta remembered his bravado when he faced the dragon with sword in hand

and then how he'd crumbled like a coward without it. She noticed he'd placed it back in the sheath attached to his belt. Thinking about him curled up in the dirt made her feel brave. "I'm curious about how such a creature came to be in the Great Turtle Lands. After all the legends I've heard, I'm guessing that must be a dragon."

Finehurst gave her a placating smile. "That's nothing to worry your pretty head about. Let's go back inside. I hadn't finished with our tour."

Weeks ago, Greeta might have agreed and smiled. After all, Finehurst had spoken words of love and promised they could have a future together. A future the men in her own village had proven she wouldn't have with any of them. Finehurst was her last chance at real happiness. Her only chance.

But a fire still burned inside her.

Greeta returned his placating smile. "That would be lovely. But this is such a wonderful opportunity for me to learn something new."

Finehurst laughed long and hard. "Why should learning anything matter to you?

You don't need to learn anything other than what I need from you." He smirked. "And all the ways I'd like you to please me."

Greeta bristled as a realization struck her.

All he cares about is what I can do for him!

She remembered the stories Papa and Auntie Peppa had told her about wealthy people in the Northlands. People with riches could afford to pay others to be in service to them.

That's how Finehurst sees me. He thinks I can be his servant.

The spirit of Margreet whispered again in Greeta's ear: *Give him no reason to suspect what you think. Not now. Not yet.*

Perhaps Margreet was right. This new realization took Greeta by so much surprise that she wanted to think about what to do next. She placed a hand on Finehurst's arm, mostly because she wanted to see how he would respond. "I suppose you're right."

Finehurst tensed at her touch and then relaxed, drawing forward to kiss her forehead. "That's my good girl."

Greeta resisted the urge to grimace. And yet a deep craving to have children and a husband still gnawed at her.

A new thought struck her.

Maybe this is the price I have to pay to get what I want. Maybe this is the price every woman has to pay.

She forced herself to smile at Finehurst.

But Auntie Peppa never had to pay that price. Uncle Killing Crow always treats her with kindness and respect. All Shining Star men are good to their wives. Even Animosh's husband treats her well.

Torn between her deepest heart's desire to have a family of her own and concern for the cost of that desire, Greeta let Finehurst lead her back into his mansion carved into the mountainside, resisting the temptation to break free and follow the path of the captured dragon.

CHAPTER 26

That night Greeta slept alone in the room Finehurst had given to her. Once asleep, she entered the Dreamtime.

Greeta dreamed she walked in the cool waters of the bay by her village. Looking out to the horizon, she saw a Northlander ship. Even this far away she could see its dragon head carved in wood.

"Beautiful, is it not?" Margreet said, walking next to her.

"I sailed on a ship like that once," Greeta said.

"As did I." Margreet sighed and smiled.

"I can't remember it," Greeta said. "I was too young to remember."

"When I sailed, it was with your mother," Margreet said. "She spoke Northlander, and I spoke Midlander. We could not understand the words we spoke." Margreet laughed. "And yet we understood each other quite well. Your mother made me very angry at times, and yet we ended up becoming friends."

"Friends?" Greeta said.

"Quite good friends." Margreet winked. "We still are."

"Margreet!" a voice called behind them.

Turning, Greeta saw the same woman she'd first seen in the grand hall when Margreet had taught her how to use a sword. Petite, dark haired, and dark skinned like the people of the Shining Star Nation. But the woman still stood so far away that Greeta couldn't see what her face looked like. "Who is she?"

The woman hesitated and then backed away toward the trees at the edge of the beach.

Margreet kept walking. "Someone you are not yet ready to meet."

Puzzled, Greeta hustled to keep up with Margreet. "I don't understand. How can I not be ready to meet someone?"

"You have not come into yourself yet. Who you truly are."

"Of course I have! I'm a grown woman."

Margreet stepped in front of Greeta, stopped, and turned to face her. "But have you not felt something new lately? A fire in your belly?"

Greeta froze, startled by Margreet's keen observation.

How does she know?

All at once, Greeta felt inadequate because Wapiti had betrayed her. Didn't that mean she wasn't good enough for the man she'd loved all her life? She felt confused by Finehurst's attention. One minute he practically begged to marry her, the next he treated her as if she were beneath him.

"I do not speak of the men in your life," Margreet said. "I speak of your conversation with the dragon."

"I don't know what you mean," Greeta stammered, worried and embarrassed that Margreet either had the ability to understand every expression on Greeta's face or had the ability to read her mind. Greeta wanted to crawl into the sand and hide in order to keep her thoughts secret and private.

"You spoke to a dragon. Not many would attempt such a thing. Why did you do it?"

Greeta thought back to what had happened. "I thought it was going to kill Finehurst, and I didn't want him to die." She hesitated, thinking about the words she'd just said and corrected herself. "I don't want him to die. I knew I couldn't run outside in time to stop the dragon from killing him. I couldn't jump out the window because it's too high. I would have hurt myself, and then I'd be no good to anybody. The only thing I could think of was to talk to the dragon. I thought maybe I could get its attention long enough for Finehurst to get away."

"I see," Margreet said, still standing in front of Greeta and blocking her path. "But the dragon spoke back."

"No!" Greeta said. "The dragon didn't talk. No animal can talk. Only people talk."

"Mmm." Margreet walked forward again, nodding for Greeta to join her side. "But the dragon understood you. And I believe you understood the dragon."

Greeta laughed. "No, I did not!"

"You told the dragon to leave Finehurst alone. You told the dragon the man is yours. And the dragon was surprised."

Greeta shrugged it off. "Maybe it was my voice that surprised it. Maybe I just interrupted it."

"You told the dragon it had no reason to be there, and that distressed the creature."

"Or maybe I made it angry because I interrupted it."

Margreet shook her head, dismissing the thought. "You accused the dragon of being a killer of men, and the dragon denied it by showing anger and distress. You accused it of being a thief, of coming to steal food. And the dragon denied your accusations yet again."

Greeta remembered the way the dragon had looked at her. Margreet was right. The dragon had denied all her allegations.

"And then you asked the dragon why it had come, and the dragon tried to explain. It tried to show you."

"I didn't understand. I couldn't.

Margreet nodded. "And yet from the moment you laid eyes upon the creature, a fire began to burn in your belly. Why do you think that is?"

Margreet spoke the truth. Greeta had

been shocked and terrified at first sight of the dragon, but then something had changed. Watching the dragon had indeed freed up something within her that Greeta had never been aware of until that moment. Talking to the dragon had flamed that hidden fire within Greeta, making her feel stronger and wiser than she'd ever felt before.

She liked it. At the same time, the change happening within made her feel uneasy. "I don't know what to do. What's happening to me?"

Up ahead, a man materialized on the beach. He stood waist deep in a large hole, digging deeper and throwing shovels of sand behind him.

"Vinchi," Margreet whispered.

"You know him?" Greeta said.

"Yes," Margreet whispered. "Along with your mother, he tried to help me. He tried to save me. But I failed to listen to him. I failed to listen to your mother. Worst of all, I failed to listen to the voice inside that would have led me to the happiness I wanted and deserved." Margreet screamed.

Startled, Greeta faced her.

Blood spread across Margreet's simple linen dress. She clutched at her chest. "You think you know your heart's desire, but you do not know who you are yet."

Greeta reached toward her. "Let me help! What can I do?"

"Nothing," Vinchi said, now standing next to Greeta, his face streaked with tears. "You can do nothing for those who will not listen, not even to their own good instincts."

Margreet clutched Greeta's hands, falling to her knees. "You must not make my mistake," Margreet said, now gasping for breath. "I married a man out of desperation, not good sense or love. I loved him because he treated me kindly at first but then he expected me to be his servant."

Greeta's blood ran cold, remembering she'd had the same thought about Finehurst.

"Listen to the guide inside you. And listen to me when I whisper in your ear!"

Margreet's grasp relaxed, and she collapsed on the ground.

Vinchi wept, sinking to his knees and holding Margreet's dead body in his arms.

Greeta woke up screaming.

CHAPTER 27

No one heard her scream.

Greeta sat up in the beautiful bed, terrified by her walk in the Dreamtime. More than ever, she wished the shaman Shadow could be here to help her make sense of it.

Remember what Margreet told you about the dragon. Remember what she said about the fire in your belly.

Greeta recognized that this was what Margreet had talked about. Perhaps they were Greeta's own thoughts from someplace deep inside, maybe even the same place where the fire in her belly had started. Perhaps she heard the voice of some kind of spirit guide inside her head. The Shining Star people believed in spirit guides, although Greeta had never had a reason to believe in them until now.

Perhaps it didn't matter whether the thoughts were Greeta's own or came from some kind of outside force. What Margreet had impressed upon her was the urgency of listening to those thoughts.

"I will listen to you," Greeta whispered. "I know I have to trust whatever you say. And I make this promise to you: from this day forward, tell me what to do and I will do it."

Then remember what Margreet said.

"She said I talked to the dragon, and the dragon talked to me," Greeta said. She kept her voice quiet, just to be especially sure no one could hear her from the hallway outside her room. "But when I told Finehurst, he laughed it off."

And why do you think he might do such a thing?

"Because he's not the man I hoped he might be," Greeta said, hearing the bitterness in her own voice. "Because he treats me like a plaything for his own amusement, not like someone who has opinions that matter."

And why else do you think he might do

such a thing?

Greeta shrugged. "I don't know. After all, it's not like I've known him all my life, the way I've known Wapiti. I only met Finehurst yesterday. I only spoke with him for an afternoon. I hardly know anything about him." Greeta snorted. "But I feel I know him as well as I know Wapiti. How can you ever know a man's true nature?" She paused, waiting for the voice to speak again. "Don't you think?"

I think you should answer the question: why do you think Finehurst would dismiss you so easily? What did he have to gain? What happened before he dismissed you?

Greeta thought back to yesterday's chain of events. "When I stood upstairs in the window, I distracted the dragon long enough that Finehurst and the Shining Star people could capture it. Then I ran downstairs and outside where they were guiding the dragon into a part of this place I haven't seen yet." Greeta sat up taller. "I told Finehurst I'd like to see the dragon, and that's when he pushed what I wanted aside. That's when he said he'd rather keep showing me his home and that I wasn't to worry about the dragon."

And what does that mean?

Anger kindled itself into a fresh flame. "It means he doesn't want me to see it."

And what do you want to do about that?

Greeta smiled. "I want to see the dragon." She waited for the voice to comment but heard nothing. Apparently, their conversation had ended for now.

After putting on a fresh buckskin dress that had been placed in her room, Greeta wound her way through the maze-like passageways of Finehurst's mansion. She focused on pretending that she belonged, nodding and smiling to Shining Star people she passed inside.

Reaching the entrance, she stepped outside, casting a gaze around the courtyard to make sure she didn't see Finehurst. Satisfied, she crossed the yard to the far right side of the mountain face to the entrance where the dragon had been guided.

Greeta studied the courtyard dirt as she walked upon it. The sharp claw marks and large smudges left from yesterday's struggle showed the direction in which the dragon had been forced. Looking ahead, she noticed a long drag mark in the dirt adjacent to the mountain and the large rock slab that now covered most of the entrance.

This time she recognized her own thoughts. *That's why I didn't notice this entrance when I first arrived yesterday! After pushing the dragon inside, they slid this slab to keep it there!*

Two light-skinned Shining Star men who appeared to be Greeta's age guarded the entrance. That meant they were Finehurst's sons. The slab left a narrow space where Greeta could easily squeeze inside. However, one of Finehurst's sons stood directly in front of that space.

She stopped in front of him. "I'd like to see the dragon."

The guard shook his head.

Greeta drew up her courage. "Finehurst told me I could. His order is for you to let me inside."

The other guard said, "That's a lie." To his brother, he said, "Don't let her in."

"It is not a lie," Greeta said, thinking indignant thoughts to make herself sound convincing. "Did you know Finehurst wants to marry me? That means I could be your mother soon. You'd better obey me now or you'll be sorry later."

The guards exchanged amused expressions and laughed.

Greeta felt the fire in her belly grow, making her feel determined and strong. She rushed forward, pushing her way around the guard and through the entrance. The darkness inside blinded her. She reached to the side until she touched the slab behind her and used it as a guide to slip out of the narrow edge of light that fell on the ground from the outside and into the darkness within.

"Stop!" The man she'd slipped past stumbled inside, equally blinded. Reaching to each side, he called out, "I can't find her!"

Overwhelmed with equal feelings of terror at being caught and exhilaration at finding what she wanted, Greeta noticed a faint glow to her left. Taking care to step softly, she edged away from the guard searching for her. She let one hand trail along the slab behind her and then along a wall that felt more like a natural cave than something that had been carved.

Another guard stepped inside, standing in the sliver of light with his colleague. "What do you mean you can't find her?"

"She isn't here!"

"She has to be here. Where else would she go?"

Taking advantage of the cover their conversation provided, Greeta made her way toward the glow and rounded a bend in what seemed to be a passageway.

Wide enough for a dragon to walk through.

A few steps beyond the bend, Greeta noticed she could no longer see the sliver of light that fell through the narrow opening where she'd met the guards.

They won't know where I am. Now is the time to move!

No longer worried about staying quiet, Greeta hurried to follow the faint glow, which lit up the passageway enough for her to find her way. The passageway snaked one way and then the next, gradually descending. She suspected it led beneath Finehurst's mansion.

In the distance, Finehurst cried out, his voice echoing as if he'd followed the guards inside. Most likely, all of them now searched for her.

There's no time to waste.

The glow had become strong enough

and Greeta's eyes had adjusted so that she could easily see the uneven stone floor and walls of the passageway. So she ran deeper and deeper underground.

Finally, the passageway opened into a huge cavern lit by a pool of molten fire at its center.

Astonished by the sight, Greeta moved toward it, aware of the heat it generated and already wiping sweat from her forehead. The molten fire bubbled inside what appeared to be a shallow pit, creeping toward its edge but never rising above it. She stared into its wondrous colors: yellow so bright that it bordered on white, dotted with black caps of crust that trembled as the fire heaved like a living, breathing thing.

Although sweat still beaded on Greeta's forehead, her feet felt chilled.

Heat rises.

She felt waves of warmth swirling all around. Looking up at the cavern's high ceiling, she thought about something Finehurst had told her: during the winter, the Shining Star people live in his mansion.

No wonder. This fire probably keeps it

warm no matter how cold it is outside.

A nearby groan made her jump in surprise.

The brightness of the fire had blinded Greeta almost as much as her first step into darkness. Now her eyes adjusted even more, but the movement of a large tail brought the creature into focus from where it blended with the color of the cave, mere steps away.

Gleaming in the fire light, the dragon's eyes looked at her with a forlorn expression, seeming to sag with hopelessness.

Greeta froze, staring at the creature, fearful it would attack and eat her.

But as her eyesight adjusted even more, Greeta saw the dragon had been tied up so that it couldn't move.

The dragon nodded its head and then looked away. Moments later, it looked back at Greeta and repeated the same motion: nodding its head and looking away, over and over again.

Greeta remembered her most recent walk in the Dreamtime and how Margreet had reinforced her thought that it was possible to communicate with a dragon. Up until now, it seemed Greeta had been successful in making herself understood but not in understanding whatever the dragon had tried to tell her.

What does it mean? Why is it nodding and then looking away? Is it agreeing with me? But about what? And why should it turn its head away?

A new thought struck her.

What if it's trying to get my attention? What if it's asking me to set it free?

Greeta circled the dragon, keeping a safe distance. When she spoke, she kept her voice low. No need to help Finehurst and the guards find her. "Are you saying you want me to help you get out of here?"

The dragon paused, staring at her. Then, with all its strength, the animal heaved itself up enough to turn slightly, away from Greeta. It nodded its head in the direction in which it turned.

Taking another step to follow, Greeta finally understood what the dragon strived to tell her.

Dozens of eggs clustered in a niche not too far from the fire.

CHAPTER 28

Stunned, Greeta looked the dragon, which now returned her gaze. "This is a hatchery," Greeta said.

Seemingly relieved, the dragon rested its jaw on the floor.

Greeta took another tentative step toward it, remembering Uncle Killing Crow's stories about bears that respected mortals and those that killed them. Although unable to tell the dragon's gender by sight, Greeta made an assumption. "Sister Dragon."

The animal lifted its jaw and glared at her.

Startled, Greeta wondered if she'd guessed wrong. "Brother Dragon?"

It snorted approval and rested its jaw

on the ground again.

"Brother Dragon. I suspect these eggs are yours and that you need help saving your children." She paused, considering the situation. "Why haven't they hatched yet? Or maybe you knew they were here and you're trying to help your own kind. Maybe Finehurst killed their parents."

The dragon struggled against the ropes binding it.

Greeta knelt, wondering how much the creature could communicate. She placed a steady hand on top of one of its paws. "Maybe I can help you. But why would Finehurst keep a hatchery of dragon eggs?"

The animal snorted in disgust but allowed Greeta's hand to stay in place.

"Yours is not to question but to obey," Finehurst said behind her.

Letting go of the dragon, Greeta spun to see Finehurst standing at the passageway, flanked by his guards. She stared at him for several long moments.

Striding forward, Finehurst swept her into his arms, holding her close and kissing her deeply.

Astonished, Greeta let him. She responded to his kiss, gentle and persistent. The warmth and pressure of his body against hers reminded her that everything she desired embraced her. All her dreams were within easy grasp.

Sinking into Finehurst's arms, Greeta remembered that the village she'd called home no longer welcomed her. Wapiti had rejected her, and no other man wanted her. If she returned, she'd spend the rest of her days living under her father's roof, and what would she do when he died? What would she do when Auntie Peppa and Uncle Killing Crow died? Would the others cast her out at a time when she'd be old and alone?

Fear clenched Greeta's belly, making her queasy. Finehurst was her final and only chance at happiness. If she didn't marry him, she'd never have another chance at being a wife and mother. She'd live her life without knowing the joy of having children. She'd never feel loved or desired again, ever. How could she say no to him?

Careful, Margreet's voice whispered in her ear. *You could end up in a far worse life than you can imagine.*

Greeta clung to Finehurst, kissing him with passion, too afraid to let him go.

You don't know him, Margreet's voice whispered. *You don't know what kind of man he is or what he is capable of doing. Although perhaps you should ask the dragon.*

The dragon. Just thinking about it shifted something inside her. Recalling how she'd felt when she saw it for the first time changed her perspective. And knowing the dragon had been bound and its mate's eggs stolen made Greeta consider that there might be matters more urgent than her own worries. Matters like protecting her family from Finehurst. Maybe even other matters that she didn't understand yet.

A new flame kindled, casting light upon her worries until they withered. Greeta shrugged off her fear and weakness like a snake shedding its skin.

Be strong, Margreet whispered, louder this time. *Have faith in yourself.*

Greeta broke away from Finehurst, holding him at arm's length. She searched his face, wondering if he'd heard Margreet's voice, too.

Instead, he seemed puzzled. "Don't you want to be my wife? Don't you want to be loved and cherished?"

Greeta remembered what Margreet had told her in the Dreamtime last night.

You must not make my mistake. I married a man out of desperation, not good sense or love. I loved him because he treated me kindly at first but then he expected me to be his servant.

Behind Greeta, the dragon groaned.

"Dragons lived across the sea in places like the Northlands," Greeta said. She crossed her arms. "What is a dragon doing here?"

Finehurst held his hand out to her, gesturing for her to take it. When she didn't, he let it fall to his side. "There are dragons in the far south of the Great Turtle Lands. It must have traveled up from there. Maybe lost its way."

The dragon groaned louder.

Margreet whispered in her ear again.

Keep your eyes on the man, not the dragon.

Greeta took the advice. Crossing her arms, she kept a steady gaze on Finehurst even when startled by the sound of a thrashing tail behind her. "And what about these eggs? This is a male dragon, not a female. Where did the eggs come from?"

The light from the molten fire pit glowed on Finehurst's face but also cast shadows into its lines, making him look old and haggard. "You need not concern yourself with any of this. All you need to think about is how happy you'll be as my wife. How happy we'll be together for the rest of our lives. Isn't that what every woman wants? A good husband and children? Don't you want to have your own happy family?"

Before his words could tempt her, Greeta remembered blood spreading across Margreet's chest. Finehurst was right. Greeta did want her own happy family. But at what cost? And if the price ended up being too high, how likely would her family be happy?

Terrified at the thought she might be destroying any chance for happiness and not knowing whether she wanted to know the truth, Greeta knew she had to forge ahead. Seeing a dragon for the first time in her life had stirred something deep inside her, and she could feel that unknown rising up through her body, making her brave. "I want to know the truth about this dragon and the eggs. I expect you to tell me the truth right now."

She heard the dragon scratch its claws against the ground behind her. The sound made her skin itch.

Finehurst's expression sagged in disappointment, and he shook his head sadly. He ducked low as he stepped forward, hauling Greeta over his shoulder and heading toward the passageway.

"No!" Greeta cried out, kicking and wriggling while Finehurst carried her through the passageway, and the guards walked behind. No matter how hard she tried to free herself, Finehurst's strong grip held her in place. She thought she inhaled his frustration, and it left a rancid taste at the back of her mouth. Her skin itched unbearably, making Greeta wish she could crawl out of it.

Minutes later, Finehurst carried her through the opening and back outside into the courtyard. The guards pushed the slab back in place to cover the entrance so no one could access it.

Finehurst leaned forward, depositing Greeta on her feet.

The fire in her belly exploded.

"Who are you to capture an animal and its young?" she shouted, jabbing an accusing finger in his face. "Who are you to come to the Great Turtle Lands and disrespect the people and the animals who are now my brothers and sisters?"

Finehurst remained calm. "I have disrespected no one."

Greeta winced at the sting of sweat that dripped into her eyes. When had she begun to perspire so profusely? At the same time, she noticed a deepening ache in her teeth and bones. Ignoring the sensation, she pointed at every light-skinned Shining Star man and woman she spotted. "You father children but you don't take any woman as your wife. How can you call that respect?"

Keeping his voice low, Finehurst said, "I have already explained that to you."

"Truly?" Greeta said, her anger building like a fire coming into its roar. She turned to face the Shining Star people. Still shouting, Greeta said, "He told me a Red Rock tribe attacked and killed many young men. He said he offered young women comfort and gave them the children they wanted. Is that what happened?"

No one replied, but the confusion on their faces concerned Greeta.

"Enough!" Finehurst said, striding forward and taking her by the arm.

Greeta dug her heels into the ground, determined to let him take her nowhere. In that moment, the earth seemed to shudder beneath her feet. It felt peculiar, but she had no time to waste on such a small thing. She needed to talk to the Shining Star people and get the truth about Finehurst. Meeting his angry gaze, she said, "Let go of me."

Finehurst grinned without humor. "Trust me. You'd rather be my wife than my enemy."

Greeta closed her eyes at the sudden heat rushing through her body. It made her feel strong and vital and powerful. Confidence made her smile at Finehurst when she said, "Let me go or I'll make you regret it." Awash with a strange desire to demonstrate her strength, Greeta opened her mouth and bared her teeth.

But her legs buckled, and she dropped

to the ground, hearing a strange ripping sound.

Finehurst shrieked and backed away, his eyes bugging out of his head.

The world changed. Finehurst looked taller but somehow smaller and weaker at the same time. A wealth of scents overwhelmed Greeta. The depth and staleness of the dirt beneath her. The crisp freshness of the air drifting from the tree lines. The tangy scent of mortal flesh, each one as unique and peculiar as its owner. The irresistible heady smell of cattle.

The Shining Star people screamed, some running inside the mansion while others climbed rocks and hid behind them.

Hunger gnawed at Greeta's belly, now dragging against the ground as she walked on all fours, unable to stand up.

I'm so hungry I could swallow an entire cow.

Startled by her own thought, Greeta wondered why it seemed so difficult to stand. Her tongue flicked out of her mouth, tasting all the glorious scents in the air.

"Sorceress!" Finehurst cried out, pointing at Greeta.

Befuddled, she said, "I'm no sorceress!"

But instead of hearing her own voice, she heard a growl.

Startled by the sound, Greeta looked down at herself and only then realized she had transformed into a dragon.

CHAPTER 29

Greeta saw her dragon legs, stumpy and bowed out to the side, ending in paws and sharp, curved talons. Looking back, she saw her long tail whipping back and forth, her scales gleaming in the sunlight.

What have you done to me? You have no right to change me!

Filled with rage and focus, Greeta stepped toward Finehurst, dragging the back of each paw against the ground before flipping it upright.

"We proceed as always," Finehurst shouted, composing himself. "All men to their positions!"

Greeta gave in to the urge to stalk Finehurst, keeping him squarely in sight.

What kind of magician are you, and why

did you do this to me? Did you do it to the dragon I saw in your fire pit? Did you change a man into a beast so you could imprison him there? You may not have him coming after you, but you've got me.

And I will make you sorry you ever thought of turning me into a dragon.

Strangely, Finehurst burst out in sweat. He spoke as if trying to placate her. "There is no need to get upset. I have no reason to harm you, and you have no reason to harm me."

No reason! Look what you've done to me!

Greeta charged and snapped her dragon jaw at him.

Fumbling, Finehurst withdrew his sword and pointed it at her snout before she could get close enough to bite him.

She stopped, startled by the sharpness of the iron point confronting her. At the same time, she flicked her long yellow tongue, tasting Finehurst's fear in the air.

"I believe this would be a good time for us to consider our options," Finehurst said with a trembling voice. He cleared his throat, striving to steady it. "You failed to mention that you have the ability to shapeshift into a dragon. Perhaps I can forgive that trespass on my trusting nature."

Enraged, Greeta hauled herself upright, standing on her hind legs until she towered above Finehurst. But that stance drained her energy, and Greeta returned to all fours.

Impossibly, Finehurst's eyes widened even more. "All right! Perhaps I expect too much from a sorceress such as you. But if you return to your mortal form, we could discuss the matter. You could tell me why you're here. What you want. Perhaps you came seeking my help, and I would be more than happy to offer such help to you."

Greeta paced from one side to another, moving closer to Finehurst each time. Pouncing forward, she batted his hands with her paw, startling him enough so that he unwittingly let go of his sword. The weapon thudded across the courtyard, landing far out of Finehurst's reach.

Whipping her tail back and forth, Greeta closed in on him.

"Now!" Finehurst shouted.

Before Greeta could pounce again, she

felt ropes latch around her legs. They pulled taut, yanking her legs out from beneath her. She slammed belly first on the ground, and men's voices yelled in triumph.

Looking to either side, she saw several Shining Star men securing the ropes against her legs. Otherwise, the courtyard had emptied. Most likely, everyone else had sought safety inside the mountain mansion.

Greeta struggled, writhing against the ropes binding her. But instead of freeing herself from them, she only managed to tighten them against her dragon flesh.

Finehurst sauntered across the yard to retrieve his sword. Face smug, he twirled it in his hands while approaching Greeta. "You thought you could outwit me?"

Greeta held herself still, knowing she would only make it easier for him to control her if she moved. Instead, she studied his every move, determined to find a way to escape.

Holding his sword up in the sunlight, Finehurst admired its sharp edges. "No one outwits me." Seeming to talk to himself, he added, "Not since the day a girl blacksmith cheated me out of everything."

His words caught Greeta's attention. Forgetting he couldn't understand her, she responded.

My mother was a blacksmith.

Instead of words, all that escaped her mouth was a roar. Even though Greeta knew little about her mother, she'd always known both her father and mother had been blacksmiths in the Northlands. They had met because of it.

Finehurst laughed. "Does my new acquisition have something to say?" He pointed the sword at her face. "Spit it out."

Furious, Greeta resisted the urge to struggle. Every word out of Finehurst's mouth convinced her that Margreet's warnings about him had been dead right. How could Greeta have been so foolish to think such a man could love her? She shuddered at how close she'd come to letting him convince her to join his side. Neither her family nor the Shining Star people in her village would ever treat any animal with this kind of disrespect. And everyone knew that the way anyone treats an animal is likely to be the same way they treat fellow mortals.

I hope the blacksmith you speak about was my mother! I hope she saw you for what you are and taught you a lesson you'll never forget!

Greeta bared her dragon teeth, rows and rows of sharp, jagged things.

Finehurst laughed. "This is a fine time to threaten me." Looking beyond her, he said to the Shining Star guards, "Go. Leave her to me. Take everyone through the mansion to the lake side. I have a private matter to conduct."

Greeta felt the ropes tugged at her legs, seemingly making sure they held her firmly in place with no chance to break free. She stared at Finehurst, unafraid. A powerful confidence surged through her dragon body, convincing her that all she had to do was keep her eyes open and be ready to grab any opportunity that presented itself.

While keeping her gaze planted firmly on Finehurst, Greeta became aware of the Shining Star men leaving the courtyard. With sharpened ears, she heard them enter the mansion and lead all of the other Shining Star people away from the courtyard side of the mansion. She listened closely, hearing their many footsteps grow faint until she could no longer hear them at all.

"Well, now," Finehurst said, sitting on the ground before her and placing the sword across his knees. "Alone at last."

Greeta flicked her tongue at him, coming close to touching the flat side of the sword.

"Fool," Finehurst said. "Don't you know even a sorceress is no match for me?"

I told you already: I am no sorceress!

Chuckling, he said, "Haven't you noticed that these Shining Star people will do anything I say? Haven't you wondered why?"

Greeta eyed him narrowly, wondering if this was why he told the others he wanted to speak with her alone.

He's gloating. He has such a grandiose opinion of himself that he needs an audience to listen to why he believes he's above everyone else. He can't bear to keep his opinion to himself. He's holding court, as if he were royalty.

"It was such a relief to meet you. You can't imagine how I've missed my own kind." Finehurst sighed. "After the first few years I came to regret the unfortunate deaths of the men who sailed here with me. Of course, they fancied themselves brigands and treated me like their thrall. They thought they were so clever to let me climb the mountainside from the lake where our ship made harbor. When they saw me climb, they thought it would be easy. Of course, they hadn't counted on the stones I threw at them from above." He shrugged. "Such a shame they lost their grip and fell to their deaths."

Greeta eyed the sword, so close and yet just out of reach. There had to be a way to trip up Finehurst.

"They didn't know I had discovered a cache of dragon eggs, wrapped each one to keep it from breaking, and stowed them on board. I couldn't let them find out. They would have destroyed them." Finehurst took his sword and dug its tip into the ground, rising to one knee. "That was their trouble. None of them knew how to think ahead to future years and the value of having dragons at your disposal."

He's breeding dragons? That means he's been doing it for as long as I've been alive. Why does no one in the Great Turtle Lands know about this?

Finehurst stood, resting both hands on top of the sword's pommel. "You saw one that escaped. Mostly, I keep them in a cave down by the lake, but that one must have found a way to climb and get out." He shook his head, perplexed. "Not sure what to do about that yet. It might be that dragon stew will be the best answer when it comes to that particular dragon."

His words made Greeta furious, and the fire in her belly raged into an inferno.

Spinning in place, Greeta whipped her tail at Finehurst, connecting hard and fast with his body. Stunned, he cried out and toppled face down while his sword clattered across the ground, far out of reach.

Continuing her momentum until she faced him again, Greeta scooped the man up between her jaws and shook him like a cat disciplining an unruly kitten.

Finehurst shrieked.

Still shaking him, Greeta sensed the ropes loosen. Perhaps all her frantic movement had made them come undone. Flinging Finehurst to one side, she shimmied, trying to work loose the ropes that bound her.

Finehurst groaned, now battered and bruised where he sprawled on the ground. He struggled to rise to one knee.

The air whistled next to Greeta's head.

Finehurst cried out and collapsed.

Looking up, Greeta saw that an arrow pierced his shoulder.

A few male voices shouted behind her, seeming to come from the field where the cows grazed. Moments later, a Shining Star man ran in front of her, holding a bow and aiming an arrow at Finehurst's heart. "Stay down."

He obeyed. Had Finehurst been standing, he would have towered above the small man.

"When you're done with her, use the bonds to tie him up," the Shining Star man said. He glanced back briefly. "What are you waiting for? Set her free."

Red Feather!

Greeta recognized the others standing behind her when they spoke.

"What if she attacks us?" Nibi said.

Returning his attention to Finehurst, now kneeling, Red Feather said, "It's Greeta. You saw her shapeshift just like I did. She's not going to hurt you."

"But she's a dragon now!" Monz said. "We don't know what dragons do."

"He's right," Finehurst chimed in. "I know dragons well, and they're very unpredictable."

"Stop talking," Red Feather said. "Unless you want this arrow in your heart." To his brothers, he said, "Cut the ropes. Now."

Greeta felt the rope around her legs grow tauter and then break loose. Within minutes she found herself free.

Red Feather, how can you be alive? I saw you killed!

But instead of hearing herself speak, Greeta heard a gentle roar.

Red Feather glanced back again to grin at her while his brothers tied up Finehurst. "It's good to see you, too, Greeta." Putting away his bow and arrow, he picked up a scrap of clothing from the ground.

Greeta recognized it as part of the dress she had been wearing and realized all her clothing must have ripped apart when she transformed into her present shape.

Red Feather stuffed the remnant of her dress into Finehurst's mouth. "If you ever try to harm this woman again, even when she's a dragon, I will kill you."

Finehurst's eyes narrowed, making him look angry. But Greeta could still see terror in his eyes.

Red Feather squatted to bring himself face to face with Greeta. "We have to get out of here. The faster, the better. Are you up for a run?"

Greeta gave him an enthusiastic nod.

Red Feather grinned. "Follow me."

Greeta turned when he darted past her and saw the three brothers sprint toward the cow field. Happily, Greeta gave chase. Although her legs were stubby and bowed out to each side, she discovered her powerful muscles gave her agility and speed. Soon, she raced past the brothers. For the first time in her life, she felt wild and joyful and free.

CHAPTER 30

In her dragon body, Greeta raced to the end of the field, amused when the grazing cows paid little attention to her presence. Instead, they were more startled by the men behind her, running to catch up. Greeta stopped short when she reached the stone wall she'd climbed over so easily just yesterday when she'd been in her mortal form. Then, it had seemed a brief inconvenience. Now, it looked like an impossible obstacle towering above her.

Whooping cries of victory, Monz and Nibi bounded past her, leaping over the wall.

"Wait!" Red Feather called after them.

Greeta turned and looked up to see concern drawing tight across his face. She looked at the wall and then back at him.

Red Feather scanned the field, the sharp mountain slopes flanking it, and the wall blocking the way it funneled into the forest. "I see no other way. You have to get over the wall, Greeta."

Remembering how she'd wedged her feet into the spaces between the stones, Greeta raised a paw only to discover it was too large to fit into any space. She paced in front of the wall, whipping her tail in frustration.

Nibi returned to the wall from the other side. "Why are you taking so long?"

Red Feather placed a hand on top of the wall, studying it. "We need to find a way to get Greeta over it."

His brother heaved a weary sigh. "Her name is Dragonfly."

Red Feather drummed his fingers on top of the stone. "Her family calls her Greeta. We're the closest she has to family right now, so I'm calling her Greeta."

"Suit yourself. I'm calling her Dragon-fly." Nibi leaned over the wall. "Hey, Dra-gonfly. Why don't you jump over the wall?"

Monz joined his brother's side. He pointed at Greeta. "Look at how those legs bow out to the side. And how low she is to the ground. I doubt she can jump at all."

Distressed by his words, Greeta turned away. Was her destiny to always be different? Monz spoke the truth. Her dragon legs were short and stumpy and ugly. Why couldn't she have turned into a beautiful deer instead?

The question is how is it possible that I turned into anything at all? What happened? What's wrong with me?

She felt a hand rest on top of her head, and she looked up to see Red Feather squat next to her.

"I saw the way you stood up to that pale man," Red Feather said, his eyes as bright as the hope in his voice. "You raised yourself up and balanced on your hind legs! Do you think you could do that again?"

Greeta looked up at the brothers standing on the other side of the stone wall and understood Red Feather's intent. When she'd stood up to Finehurst, she'd towered above him. If she could figure out how to do it again, she'd tower above the wall and could make her way over it.

She backed out from under Red Feather's hand and tried to stand. Instead, she managed to only sit back on her haunches.

"She's a dragon," Nibi complained. "You can't talk to her. She can't understand."

"She only understands dragon talk now," Monz said.

"Nonsense," Red Feather said. "She recognizes what we say. But she's been in the dragon body for precious little time. She needs time to figure out how to make it work."

"Then she'd better hurry." Nibi glanced up at the position of the sun. "That pale man will find help soon, and then we'll have a fight on our hands."

Monz spoke loud and slowly, as if he were talking to a foreigner. "We found a hiding place, Dragonfly. It's a good one where they'll never find us. But you have to get over this wall before we can get there."

Greeta felt frustration rise within her. She rose from her haunches and tried to stand up again, this time making the equivalent of a miniscule leap.

"She's not a child," Red Feather said to Monz. "Don't speak to her that way. She's still our friend."

"I'm trying to help." Monz smiled and

looked beyond his brother. "You almost did it, Dragonfly. Try again!"

Taking heart from Monz's encouragement, Greeta thought back to how angry she'd felt at Finehurst. Giving her all, Greeta brought her dragon body into a standing position and staggered toward the wall until her back legs rammed into it, sending her sprawling across it.

"Well done, Greeta!" Red Feather said.

Although Greeta now faced the welcome sight of the forest, she felt her hind legs caught on the other side of the stone wall. Glancing back, she groaned in frustration.

"Help me push her over," Red Feather called out to his brothers.

Nibi and Monz hopped the wall to join their brother's side.

"I think we should grip the heel," Red Feather said. "Be careful of her claws. They look sharp enough to slice you open."

Greeta squirmed, making one more attempt to climb up the wall with her back legs.

The young men cried out in surprise.

"Relax, Greeta," Red Feather said from the other side of the wall. "Let us do the work."

Greeta understood, remembering what Red Feather had said to his brothers about her claws moments ago. She realized she had to be gentle with them and mindful of her actions. Otherwise, she might hurt the very people trying to help her.

Letting herself go limp, she felt tiny hands pushing against the bottom of her foot. If Greeta had been in her mortal body, it would have felt like squirrels nudging her soles.

To his brothers, Red Feather said, "We have to push together. Give her one good shove."

This time Greeta felt strength behind their effort and tumbled over the wall as a result. Landing on one shoulder, she rolled over until she could find the balance to bring her dragon body upright and stand. Happy to be free of the wall, she flicked her long yellow tongue, tasting the men's relief in the air.

Nibi and Monz sprinted past her, weaving their way into the forest ahead.

Red Feather placed a hand on her shoulder. "Follow us, Greeta. We've been watching that pale man and the way he controls the people around him. They will come after us. And we have to get to our hiding place before they catch up."

Red Feather bounded in his brothers' footsteps.

Greeta cast one last look behind at the field of scattered cows and the mountain mansion rising behind it. Seeing no one in the courtyard, she imagined Finehurst must have gone inside to seek help and most likely gather up his strongest men to try to capture her again. She'd seen his secret: the dragon and the eggs in the underground hatchery. Even though she didn't understand that secret, she doubted Finehurst would want her walking in the world with it on the tip of her tongue, ready to tell.

How could I have ever imagined I was in love with such a man?

Shaking her head in disgust, Greeta trotted in the direction Red Feather had taken, knowing she'd have him back in sight within moments.

CHAPTER 31

By the end of the day, the brothers and Greeta stood on the floor of a narrow chasm. Gray stone walls rose sharply, flanking them on either side. Thick bushes covered one wall, fed by a steady trickle of a stream running down that wall and forcing its way through every crack. Tall trees lined the ledges above.

Monz pointed at the opening to a small cave, so well hidden that Greeta kept losing sight of it even while staring directly at the opening. "She's too big to fit," Monz said.

"That's because we didn't know she was going to turn into a dragon," Nibi said, casting an accusing glance at her.

Greeta answered with a low growl. In

her mortal form, she probably would have pouted over feeling wounded by his words. Now things were different. Now she'd turned into something dangerous. She had no intent of harming Nibi.

But it sure was fun to throw a little bit of a scare into him.

"It's not her fault she turned into a dragon," Red Feather said.

"How do you know?" Monz said. "Maybe she did it on purpose. Maybe she's refusing to turn back into one of us because she isn't one of us."

"All right," Red Feather said. "Let's ask her." Facing Greeta squarely, he said, "Did you make yourself turn into a dragon? Was it your choice?"

Greeta growled again, this time shaking her head emphatically from side to side.

"There," Red Feather said, pointing at her. "She gave you her answer. She didn't turn into a dragon on purpose."

Nibi snorted. "Or maybe she's chasing a fly away from her nose!" He spoke to Red Feather as if he were a child. "She's a dragon. She doesn't understand a word you say."

Ignoring his brother, Red Feather took a

step closer to Greeta. "Show them they're wrong. Greeta, do you understand me?"

Now Greeta nodded her head up and down.

Red Feather smiled. "Do you want to stay in your dragon body?"

She shook her head from side to side, indicating she didn't.

Red Feather's smile broadened. "Is it your wish to take your mortal shape again?"

Greeta nodded.

Facing his brothers again, Red Feather said, "I don't know how she could make herself more plainly understood. Her father asked us to bring her back, and we promised to do so. We didn't say we'd give up if she somehow turned into a dragon along the way."

My father asked them to bring me back? Why? Did he know something had gone wrong?

Not wanting to make them think she was angry by growling again, Greeta took a small step forward and managed to make some small chirping sounds.

Startled, Nibi took a step back. "Now what does she want?"

"I don't know," Red Feather said, worry creasing his brow. "Greeta, there's no time to figure out what you want. We have to figure out how to hide before the sun goes down. We've already heard them behind us."

Greeta nodded her understanding and plopped down on her belly, resting her entire body on the cool stone surface of the chasm floor.

Red Feather disappeared into the cave for a moment. Popping back out, he said, "Greeta, there's just enough room for you to fit inside." He pointed down the chasm's length. "There are places we've seen for each one of us to take cover. Ledges cover-ed by vines or bushes. We'll leave Greeta in the cave, but we'll be close enough to help her if they find her."

Greeta propped herself up on two front legs, peering toward the cave with trepi-dation.

Seeming to read her expression, Red Feather gestured toward the cave. "It's fine, Greeta. All you have to do is squeeze up alongside the wall. You're the same color as the stone. You'll blend into it perfectly. If you keep your eyes closed, no one will ever know you're there."

A voice called out in the distance.

"They're getting close," Monz said.

"Both of you find a place to hide. I'll be right behind you." Red Feather walked to Greeta's side. "I promise we'll keep you safe."

But Greeta worried. What if Finehurst found her first? What if his men captured or killed Red Feather and his brothers? She didn't want to go into the cave because it gave her nowhere else to escape. She could be cornered so easily with no chance to run away.

Unable to speak her concerns to Red Feather, she gently placed her front paw on top of his foot, careful to keep her large, curved claws away from his flesh.

Startled to find himself pinned to the ground, Red Feather paled.

Greeta kept a firm grip on his foot.

Red Feather swallowed hard and said, "I don't understand."

Greeta nodded toward the cave and then shook her head.

"You need to hide, Greeta. There are too few of us and too many of them. We don't know this land well enough to travel in the dark. If we stay in the open, they'll find us. Our only chance is to hide. If they discover our hiding places, then we'll fight back." Leaning forward, he placed a calming hand on top of her head. "But the best way to win a fight is to avoid it altogether."

In her heart, she knew Red Feather spoke the truth. But the idea of hiding alone scared Greeta. Without thinking, she flicked her tongue, wrapping it around Red Feather's wrist for a few moments before letting go.

Red Feather shuddered, looking startled and frightened. But then his face brightened. "Would you like me to stay with you?"

Greeta nodded and lifted her paw from his foot, setting Red Feather free.

Looking up toward his brothers moving down the chasm, Red Feather waved them on. He spoke quietly, as if Finehurst and his men might be getting close enough to hear. "Here's what we will do. Let me lie between you and the wall of the cave. Press yourself up against the wall, just not so much that you crush me. If they carry torches, you will blend with the wall so much that they won't know you're there.

That's why I need to hide behind you."

Greeta nodded, realizing the light cast by a torch would reveal Red Feather immediately if he were in the open. But she knew from experience how difficult it could be to see frogs or lizards or even birds in plain sight because they blended so well with their surroundings.

She entered the cave first, barely fitting inside and lining herself against its wall. Thinking her teeth and claws might gleam in the firelight from a torch, she faced the wall. Her back would be more likely to blend in with the cave.

Red Feather crawled over her back and nestled into a space between her paws and chest.

The sensation startled her. In her dragon body, Greeta wore nothing but naked skin. The warmth of Red Feather's face rested against what would have been her naked breasts if she were in mortal form. The thought of it made her heart race.

Why do I feel this way? It's only Red Feather.

"Your heart beats fast," he said. Red Feather stroked her dragon chest. "Don't worry. I'll keep you safe." He laughed softly. "What am I saying? You're more likely to keep me safe!"

Greeta curled her tail until she could lay the tip across Red Feather's foot.

"We'll be fine, Greeta," he said. "We can help each other." Red Feather stroked her chest, lulling Greeta into such a peaceful feeling that she drifted to sleep.

Sometime later, she awoke with a start at the sound of men shouting outside the cave. At the same time, she felt Red Feather press a firm hand against her.

Greeta wanted to scream and run away, even though she had no place to run. Instead, she focused on Red Feather's calming touch and remembered their plan: to stay still and quiet, hoping Greeta would blend into the stone so much that anyone who looked inside the cave wouldn't detect her presence.

Still facing the side of the cave, Greeta's heart doubled its pace when she saw it light up with the orange glow of fire. That meant someone carrying a torch now stood at the entrance to the cave.

Finehurst's voice called from a short distance. "What do you see?"

A nearby Shining Star voice called back.

"I cannot be sure."

Greeta realized the man standing at the cave's entrance might be a warrior or a hunter, someone experienced in looking at his surroundings with a sharper eye than most. Terrified, she told herself not to tremble, not to give herself away.

At the same time, she felt Red Feather's body tense against hers, ready to spring into action and fight.

A crunch of pebbles under a simple deerskin shoe told Greeta the intruder had taken a step inside. If he kept walking toward them, he'd see Greeta's shape within moments. She and Red Feather were sure to be captured.

But then Greeta realized something else: the man entering the cave was a Shining Star man, not Finehurst. And that man most likely had the same sensibilities that Greeta had learned from the people of the Shining Star Nation.

Closing her eyes, Greeta focused on the very tip of her tail. A good length of the end of her tail was very narrow, about the width of a finger. She'd tucked it in toward the wall, but now she concentrated on moving it in the direction of the footstep, winding it from side to side.

The man let loose a quiet gasp. "Brother Snake," the man said. "I did not intend to enter your home unannounced or uninvited. Please forgive me."

His gravelly footsteps receded. He said, "There is nothing inside."

Finehurst's voice grew nearer. "Are you sure? Did you check everywhere?"

"The space is very small. It's empty, except for a snake."

Greeta kept her tail side-winding for as long as she saw the orange glow on the wall she faced, even though its presence had faded substantially. But then it glowed a little brighter.

She recognized Finehurst's voice when he cried out.

The orange glow disappeared, telling Greeta Finehurst must have poked his head inside, glimpsed her side-winding tail, and immediately retreated.

More distant now, Finehurst said, "Search everywhere. Every nook and cranny."

No one came back to the cave, but Greeta felt Red Feather's tension, knowing one or both of his brothers could be found at any moment.

But she heard no cries of success, only Finehurst's disgruntled complaints. Within a short time, all of the voices drifted away, and Greeta fell into a sleep of relief.

CHAPTER 32

The next morning, Greeta awoke alone in the cave, sprawled across its floor. She groaned and stretched, still unaccustomed to her dragon body. Hoisting her weight onto four legs, she lumbered out of the cave and into the bright light of day.

She saw no sign of Red Feather or his brothers.

They've left me!

Greeta trembled with the same wave of panic she'd felt when she'd come awake from her first walk in the Dreamtime to discover that the shaman Shadow had vanished. Why were people disappearing? Were they abandoning her? Had they been killed or captured?

Overwhelmed with anxiety, Greeta turned in a circle, looking all around her for any sign of the young men. Then she remembered she had an advantage in her dragon body that she'd never experienced as a mortal.

She flicked her long yellow tongue in the air, and tasted the essence of Red Feather and his brothers: stale sweat, weariness, and intrigue.

Intrigue?

Greeta flicked her tongue again, tasting the peculiar scents. Did the taste mean they longed for intrigue or that they had found something that intrigued them?

Heading in the direction of the scents she tasted, Greeta followed the trail they'd left in the air. She'd always thought of a scent as something to be smelled, not tasted. But her tongue picked up tastes in the air as if they hung there in suspension, ready for her to savor.

Being a dragon is very peculiar.

Continuing to flick her tongue and follow their trail, Greeta turned a corner in the chasm to discover the young men huddled around a pile of stones at the bottom of another thin stream of water trickling from high above and down the chasm wall.

Looking up, Red Feather brightened when he saw her. "Greeta, look!"

Trudging forward on her bowed legs, Greeta saw the men part and reveal a pile of eggs like the ones she'd seen in Finehurst's hatchery. Excited, she stepped forward until she could nudge them with her nose. Oddly, their heavy weight made them difficult to move.

Something isn't right.

Greeta flicked her tongue over the eggs, tasting them.

They taste like stone!

"Aren't they beautiful?" Red Feather said.

Puzzled, Greeta stared at him.

Monz picked one up, running his hands across its smooth surface. "They're rocks." He pointed upward. "This must have been a powerful waterfall for many years, and these rocks were at the bottom. The water made them tumble and wore them down until they were smooth."

"Or a stream ran through here," Nibi argued. "It's usually streams that make rocks this smooth and round. And that stream might be what carved out this chasm."

"However they were made, they're beautiful," Red Feather said.

Greeta nosed the stones again. Red Feather and his brothers were right. These were stones, not eggs. But she couldn't see the beauty in them. She could only think of how she'd found a dragon and dragon eggs being held captive by Finehurst, and his disrespect of them made her angry. She backed away from the eggs and snorted, looking toward the direction leading to Finehurst's mansion.

She could feel how being a dragon changed her. She felt compelled to help other dragons. What if they were mortals trapped in dragon bodies like hers? And wouldn't that mean the eggs might contain babies that were mortal themselves?

How can I walk away from them when they need help? Why is Finehurst keeping them prisoner? What reason could he have?

"Greeta," Red Feather said. "I don't understand what you're saying."

"That's because she's not talking, she's growling," Nibi said.

"Don't rile her up," Monz said. "She may

be Dragonfly, but she's also a dragon. And from what I've seen so far, it looks like dragons can be mighty treacherous."

We have to go back! We have to tell Finehurst to let the dragon and the eggs go. He is not a good man, and I don't trust his reasons for keeping them.

Nibi walked a few steps toward her. He spoke as if trying to reason with a child. "Dragonfly, we don't understand you because we don't speak dragon talk."

"Truly," Red Feather said to him. "Don't talk to her that way." To Greeta, he said, "But I have to admit my brother is right. We can't understand you. Can you show us what you're talking about?"

His words gave Greeta an idea. She nodded and approached the polished stones. Using her paws, she rolled several of them into the center of the chasm floor.

"What is she doing?" Monz whispered.

Nibi shrugged. "I don't know. She likes to play with stones?"

"Hush," Red Feather said. "She's not done yet."

Greeta pushed the stones together. Carefully, she sat on them in the same way she'd seen birds warm their eggs before they hatched.

Nibi scrunched his face up in confusion. "She likes to sit on stones?"

"Maybe," Monz reasoned, "if they're round and comfortable."

Greeta shook her head, rejecting their guesses. She stood on her legs again and walked around the stones before sitting on them again.

"Eggs," Red Feather said. "She's telling us something about eggs."

"Good!" Monz said. "Maybe we can eat them for breakfast."

Greeta shook her head again. Once again, she circled the stones and sat in front of them. Using her front paws, she drew the stones toward herself.

Red Feather's voice softened. "I think she's talking about dragon eggs."

Jumping to all fours, Greeta nodded.

We have to find the eggs and take them away from Finehurst!

She trotted to Red Feather and placed her nose squarely against his back, pushing him toward the collection of stones she'd gathered.

Red Feather looked at them, confused again. "But there are no dragons in the

Shining Star Nation."

Greeta stomped one paw powerfully against the ground, making it shake.

"Except for her," Nibi said, pointing at Greeta. "Dragonfly has most definitely turned into a dragon."

"Of course," Red Feather said. He paled. "Are you saying that you laid eggs?"

"She's going to have children?" Nibi shouted in amazement.

"That seems awfully sudden," Monz said. "Is there something we should know? Perhaps something involving you and Wapiti?"

Greeta stomped again, shaking her head back and forth.

Nibi looked at Monz and said, "I think you insulted her."

"It is too sudden for her to have children," Red Feather said. "Or lay eggs. There's something we do not understand."

Greeta heaved a weary sigh in agreement. Maybe it was too much to ask these brothers to help her. How could she ask them to put themselves in even greater danger than they already had? After all, she'd seen Badger Face throw Red Feather off a cliff, and she still didn't understand how he'd survived. She'd seen Nibi and Monz tied up and left for dead. And she hadn't done anything to help them. Instead, she'd become so weak and mindless that she'd allowed herself to believe she could fall in love with someone like Finehurst.

She'd let the brothers return home, and she'd face Finehurst on her own.

Greeta lowered her front legs to bow, hoping they'd understand her gratitude for all the brothers had done for her.

"What is she doing now?" Monz said.

Greeta stood back up on all four legs, turned, and trotted back in the direction from which they had come.

She heard Red Feather call out her name, but she kept trotting forward, grateful that after all the horrible experiences she'd had since the day she'd discovered Wapiti on the beach with Animosh, these brothers had treated her with a kindness she thought she'd never experience again.

Besides, they wouldn't understand the instinct that bolted through her blood. The instinct to help and protect other dragons. How could she expect the brothers to understand when she didn't understand it herself?

She didn't want them to jeopardize their lives on her behalf again. Greeta ran, knowing she'd reach Finehurst's mansion long before Red Feather and his brothers would be able to catch up with her.

CHAPTER 33

Greeta back-tracked, surprised at how much easier it was to find her way as a dragon than she had as a mortal. Scents hung like signposts, filling her path with information. She trotted through the forest, flicking her tongue and tasting a wealth of details: Finehurst's bitter anger, the bland dismay of his Shining Star minions, and faint traces of Red Feather, his brothers, and even her own dragon self from their earlier journey.

She marveled at how much easier her life seemed now with no need to worry about mortals accepting her. Greeta needed mortals no more. Of course, she missed Papa, Auntie Peppa, and Uncle Killing Crow. And her heart held a special place for Red Feather, Nibi, and Monz. But she had no use for anyone else. Instead, she felt an inexplicable pull toward exploring her new life as a dragon, which included a deep anxiety about the eggs in Finehurst's hatchery. She had to protect them.

What is happening to me? Why am I abandoning my mortal life so easily? Why shouldn't I fight to get my mortal body back and go home?

A sense of power surged through her, making her feel vibrancy and desire to live to a degree she'd never known before.

Maybe this is who I really am. Maybe this is who I always was.

Her own thoughts startled her. They were impossible, but at the same time felt true and right.

Greeta's stomach growled, reminding her that she'd eaten nothing since becoming a dragon. Despite her desire to confront Finehurst as soon as possible, her new body made it clear that the time had come to renew its strength by finding something to eat.

Flicking her tongue, Greeta tasted water in the air. When she stilled herself and focused, she detected the sound of a stream and things splashing inside it.

Fish!

Plowing her way through the forest, Greeta found the stream several minutes later, throwing herself in the middle of it with an open jaw. The thunder of rushing water filled her ears, but she sensed the movement of fish tumbling toward her and met them with sharp teeth. In her mortal form, Greeta had always wanted fish well cooked, but now she delighted in the experience of swallowing them whole. Within minutes she felt satisfied and climbed onto the river bank, pausing to warm herself on a rock ledge already hot in the sunlight. Relaxed, she began to drift asleep only to come awake with a start.

For a moment, Greeta thought she heard something in the distance behind her.

I have to keep going. There's no time to rest.

Shaking herself awake, Greeta retraced her steps to her original path and resumed her journey.

By mid-day she reached the forest leading to Finehurst's enclave, surprised to find several cows scattered among the trees. A chill ran through her.

Something is wrong.

Greeta crept through the forest, lingering inside its tree line when she reached the edge of the valley. Keeping her body low to the ground, she edged closer to get a better look.

The stone wall separating the forest from the field where Finehurst's cattle grazed had been knocked down.

Greeta flicked her tongue, but the air tasted empty. It made her want to turn around, to run back to Red Feather and his brothers and forget she'd ever met Finehurst.

But she couldn't leave the dragon or the eggs in his grasp. Her burning desire to help them outweighed her fear of what she might find beyond the broken wall.

Keeping her wits about her, Greeta emerged from the forest and picked her way through the rubble of the broken wall. The few cows still grazing in the field mooed in the distance before backing away as she edged along one mountainside flanking the field.

Again, staying low to the ground, she approached the courtyard, surprised to find it quiet and empty. Looking up, she saw no one standing at any of the windows. Tasting the air again, she found it dusty and stale.

I should be able to taste the presence of everyone here, even if they're inside. Unless they've gone through to the other side. Maybe Finehurst has taken them all to the lake side.

Then this would be the best time to make her way through the passageway leading below the mansion to where Finehurst kept his hatchery.

Greeta ran across the courtyard to the slab of rock blocking the entrance to the lower region. She braced one shoulder against the slab. With one mighty heave, she shoved it onto the ground, where it broke in pieces. Stepping inside, her dragon eyes adjusted quicker and more easily to the darkness than when she'd been a mortal. She retraced the steps she'd taken yesterday, this time running through the twisting passageway until she reached the cavernous room below.

Stunned, she stared at the empty space.

Maybe I took a wrong turn. Maybe this is the wrong room.

Looking back, Greeta struggled to figure out where she might have taken a misstep. It didn't make any sense.

She studied the space surrounding her, recognizing the fire pit, still burning bright. Stepping closer, she noticed a few broken shells on the ground.

They hatched!

Flicking her tongue, she tasted the scent of newly-hatched dragons, oddly sour and sweet at the same time. The taste reminded her of what she'd longed for her entire life, her dream of having a wonderful husband like Wapiti and her own children. But that dream lay as broken on the ground as the eggshells, destroyed forever and unable to be put back together.

A flame of anger stirred inside Greeta's belly. Finehurst had destroyed her life by changing her into a dragon. But she would make use of this new life. Maybe living among other mortals was never meant to be. If she couldn't find a place where she felt accepted and loved, she could at least make sure Finehurst never did this kind of harm to any other mortal or caused damage to any other dragon.

Greeta noticed a new scent, clean and pure. It stirred her curiosity, and she took a step back from the broken eggshells. She stared at them, thinking she must be missing something that might be staring her in the face.

Catching her breath, Greeta finally saw it. If she imagined piecing the eggshells together, they would have come from no more than four eggs, maybe five at the most. She'd seen far more eggs than that.

Only a few of the eggs had hatched. The other eggs had simply gone missing, along with the dragon and the hatchlings.

What is Finehurst up to?

Greeta snorted her disgust. Her anger flamed through her dragon body, burning away any fear into cinders. She didn't care about being cautious any more. She didn't care about slipping up unnoticed or taking Finehurst by surprise. She'd rather hunt him down and face him and all his people, all the Shining Star people who betrayed their nation by following him instead of their own tradition of honoring the land and all its creatures. No native of the Great Turtle Lands would ever stoop so low as to capture a dragon, much less harbor dozens of dragon eggs.

Full of determination and new purpose, Greeta stormed back through the underground passageway and back into the still empty courtyard, thrashing her tail in anger. Finehurst and his Shining Star people had to be either inside the mansion or on the other side of it, the area facing the lake where he had shown Greeta his Northlander ship in the water below.

Stomping into the mansion, Greeta growled, satisfied to hear her menacing dragon voice echo throughout the rooms. She plotted her path so that no one inside the mansion or on the other side of it would be able to escape without confronting her first.

But room after room, she found no one, not even in Finehurst's bedroom or the one he had given to her. The recent memory that she had considered sharing that bed with him and bearing his children now sickened her.

How could I have been so foolish?

But Greeta knew the answer. Even though little time had passed, she now saw the world through the eyes of a dragon, not a young woman desperate to live the safest and most comfortable life she could imagine. If she'd ignored the things she would have eventually learned about Finehurst and his underground prison, she would have ended up like his Shining Star people: having a warm place to endure each winter at the cost of ignoring Finehurst's sins.

For a moment, Greeta was glad she'd been turned into a dragon. At the same time, she wished she'd never left home, even if it meant living a life feeling sorry for herself as an undesirable woman.

But I know about Finehurst now. And I have to find him.

Greeta made quick work of checking every nook and cranny of the mansion, finding no trace of Finehurst or his people. That meant they had to be on the lake side of the mansion.

She retraced the steps she'd taken when Finehurst had led her there, growling louder this time, wanting him to know of her presence. Wanting Finehurst to know that he couldn't control or harm her, because this time she gave him no benefit of doubt and came ready to fight.

Emerging from the mansion carved into

the mountain, Greeta blinked at the brightness of the sun, but her vision adjusted quickly.

She found the ledge empty, so she looked around to make sure no one hid or had climbed on the face of the mountain behind her, ready to ambush. Still, she stood alone.

Creeping to the edge of the cliff, she looked down at the lake.

Its shores and the lake itself stood empty. Finehurst's ship had vanished.

CHAPTER 34

They're gone. Finehurst has taken his people and disappeared with them. And he must have taken that dragon and the eggs with him.

Greeta's dragon body collapsed to the ground. She wanted to cry but discovered she couldn't.

There must be something I can do. I have to tell people about Finehurst. I have to tell them what I know. But how?

She stared at the sky above, searching for clarity in its cloudless blue color, deep and bright. She retraced her journey, thinking about how Red Feather and his brothers had freed her, how she'd thought she might love Finehurst when he made advances toward her, how Badger Face had thrown Red Feather off a cliff, how she'd wandered to Badger Face's village, only to feel even more rejected than she had in her own village.

And how she'd traveled with the shaman Shadow, who had led Greeta to walk in the Dreamtime.

Blinking at the sky above, Greeta felt struck by a realization.

Since the first time Shadow led me into the Dreamtime, I've gone there on my own. I've spent time with Margreet there. She taught me how to fight with a sword.

Can I still enter the Dreamtime now that I'm a dragon?

Deciding to take a leap of faith, Greeta closed her eyes and let herself drift asleep in the warmth of the sun.

CHAPTER 35

Greeta found herself on board a Northlander ship, sailing at sea.

I've made it! I'm back in the Dreamtime!

The Northlander ship stretched long and narrow, skimming so low through the waves that Greeta thought if she dared to lean over the rail, she could touch the saltwater. Oars were stored stacked up in the center of the deck, and an enormous single square sail billowed above. Men scurried, tending to the sail and maintaining the ship's course.

"How lovely that you could join us," Margreet said.

Greeta turned to see Margreet leaning on the rail, staring out toward the sea. Happiness rushed through Greeta, thrilled to see Margreet alive and whole again. But Greeta worried about how to make herself understood. If Red Feather and his brothers couldn't understand Greeta, how could Margreet? But she had to try, because she could think of nothing else to do.

"Margreet, look at me! Someone turned me into a dragon!"

Margreet laughed, turning her back on the sea and facing Greeta. "I think not. Look at yourself."

Greeta realized that instead of looking up at Margreet, she stood at eye level with her. Looking down at herself, Greeta saw her mortal body. "I'm myself again!"

"You always were," Margreet said, smiling.

Greeta wrapped her arms around herself, happy to feel the texture of the buckskin dress she wore at home. "I don't understand."

A man approached, and Greeta recognized him as Vinchi, who had been digging a hole in the sand when she'd last walked in the Dreamtime. He wrapped an arm around Margreet's shoulders, and pulled her close. Margreet smiled, closing her eyes for a moment as she nestled her head against his shoulder. "I was happy on this ship," Margreet said. "I didn't know it at the time, but I had so much to be happy about."

"Please," Greeta said. "I need help."

An unfamiliar voice said, "You already have it." The woman Greeta had glimpsed when she'd first met Margreet in the Dreamtime stood a short distance behind Vinchi and Margreet. Greeta remembered being surprised by her appearance in the hall where Margreet had taught her how to use a sword, because the woman's skin and hair were dark, making her look like a native of the Great Turtle Lands, unlike the pale-skinned and fair appearance of Margreet, Vinchi, and everyone else on board the Northlander ship.

Turning slightly, Vinchi reached a hand out to the strange woman, and she stepped forward to take it, joining his side.

"I don't understand," Greeta said, still comforted by the feeling of her own arms wrapped around her body. "How can I already have help when in my world I'm a dragon that no one can understand? I can't go back home. I have no friends. No family."

"That's not true," the strange woman said. "You have your father. Peppa. Even her husband, the man who kills crows."

Greeta laughed. "He doesn't kill crows. It's just his name. Uncle Killing Crow."

"And you have me," the strange woman said. "I'm your mother."

Stunned by her words, Greeta stared. "That's impossible. My mother was a Northlander. A blacksmith like my father. I was with him when he sailed across the great ocean. He couldn't have taken a Shining Star wife."

"I am a Northlander. And a blacksmith. And your mother." The woman's appearance shifted, her black hair fading to blonde, her dark skin lightening shades paler than Margreet's skin.

But the most disturbing sight to Greeta was the dozens of ragged scars covering the woman's pale skin. "What happened to you?"

"My family," the woman said. Her voice took a depth of sadness. "I don't understand why you're not grateful for what you already have. You are surrounded by people who love you and will do anything to help and protect you. And we're with you every day. I'm by your side every day. I'm by your father's side, too."

Greeta reeled in confusion. "But my Papa sent me away with a shaman."

"For your own benefit," the woman said. "He suspects what you already have inside you, and he knew you needed guidance from someone who could help."

"But everyone in my village. They hate me. They don't want me there. I can't go back."

Margreet laughed, "Nonsense!"

The strange woman sighed. "Open your eyes to the truth. You're letting a few disappointments cloud your vision."

"But I'm a dragon when I'm not here! Who turned me into a dragon? Why did it have to happen to me?"

The woman who claimed to be Greeta's mother stepped toward her with out-stretched hands.

Standing tall above her, Greeta tentatively placed her hands in them. A shiver ran through her body. Looking closer at the woman's face, Greeta noticed that although her features hadn't changed, they had the narrowness of a Northlander's face, like Auntie Peppa's, not the broadness of the face of a native of the Great Turtle Lands.

CHAPTER 36

Greeta awoke with a start, feeling something land on top of her chest.

"My eyes are closed," Red Feather said.

Greeta blinked against the bright sun, feeling disoriented, not sure whether she'd come back to her own world or if she'd simply landed in another space in the Dreamtime. She blinked again, irritated that her vision took so long to adjust to the light.

Propping herself up on her elbows, Greeta squinted at Red Feather, standing at her feet. Finally, her eyes adjusted enough so that she could see he stood shirtless and with both hands covering his eyes. "What happened to your shirt?"

When Red Feather spoke, his hands

muffled his voice. "I gave it to you."

"Why?"

"Because you're naked." Red Feather took one hand away and pointed at her, his eye open, widening at the sight of her. He closed it quickly, covering his face with both hands again. "I'm sorry! I'm not looking!"

For the first time, Greeta looked at herself. "I'm myself again!"

"That's what I've been trying to tell you," Red Feather said, his voice muffled once more by the hands clapped over his face.

Greeta realized Red Feather was right. He'd thrown his buckskin shirt on top of her, but she didn't have a stitch of her own clothing on. When she spoke, she heard suspicion creep into her voice. "How did this happen to me?"

"I don't know. But I suspect that when you turned into a dragon, you ripped through your own clothing. Because you were naked when you were a dragon." Red Feather hesitated, sounding more nervous by the moment. "I've never seen a dragon before, but I don't think they wear clothes."

Greeta scrambled onto her knees,

gathering Red Feather's shirt in her hands. "Where are your brothers?"

"Searching inside." Red Feather's tone shifted into curiosity. "How did they carve this place out of a mountain?"

Squeezing herself into Red Feather's shirt, Greeta stood up. "I'm dressed."

"Good." Red Feather opened his eyes, only to look mortified and covered them again. "No, you're not."

Looking down, Greeta saw that his shirt fell only as far as her waist. Shrieking in surprise and embarrassment, she leaned forward and bent her knees, pulling on the bottom edge of the shirt to cover herself.

His eyes still closed, Red Feather said, "You forgot you're taller than me. It won't cover you the same way."

"What's wrong?" Nibi said, bursting from the lake-side entrance to the mansion. He stopped short, staring from Greeta's hunched figure to Red Feather covering his eyes and then back at Greeta. "Why are you half-naked?"

"Stop looking at me!" Greeta shouted.

"Give her your breeches," Red Feather said.

Turning to Red Feather, Nibi said, "Why

should I? Why don't you give her *your* breeches?"

"Because she already has my shirt. Yours will keep you covered."

"Who yelled?" Monz said, following in his brother's footsteps and bumping into Nibi. Pointing at Greeta, Monz said, "Why is she naked?"

"Because she changed back from being a dragon," Red Feather said. "Now somebody give her some breeches."

"Oh!" Monz brightened. "Remember how naked she was when she was a dragon?" He nodded his understanding. "She's still naked." Happily he took off his breeches and tossed them at Greeta, where they landed at her feet. Punching Nibi in the arm, he said, "Turn around and give the girl some privacy."

"Fine," Nibi said, taking one last glimpse at Greeta before following his brother's orders. "But it's not like we haven't seen her without any clothes before."

"But that's when she was a dragon," Red Feather said. "It's different now."

"I don't know," Nibi said. "Naked is naked."

Satisfied that none of the three brothers

was watching, Greeta slipped on Monz's breeches, happy to discover they fit. "Thank you," she said.

The brothers faced her again, Red Feather letting his hands fall away from his face. "How did you change back?"

Greeta hesitated, not sure she wanted to tell them about how Shadow had taught her to enter the Dreamtime or what she'd learned while there. She realized she could tell the truth without mentioning the Dreamtime. "I don't know. When I laid down to rest, I was a dragon. When Red Feather woke me up, I was like this."

Monz nudged Nibi in the ribs. Smiling mischievously, Monz said, "Except for the naked part."

"Thank you," Greeta said, remembering what the woman who claimed to be her mother had told her. "I'm grateful for the clothes."

Red Feather grinned. "I'm grateful to see you again. What happened? We saw you change into a dragon, but we couldn't see how you did it."

Greeta stared at him in surprise. "I didn't do it! Finehurst must have turned me into a dragon."

"I don't think so," Nibi said. "Didn't you notice how surprised he looked when it happened?"

Greeta hesitated. Nibi spoke the truth. Finehurst had appeared shocked, and why would that happen unless he'd been as surprised as Greeta when she turned into a dragon? "Then I don't know how it happened. But you were watching?"

Monz nodded. "After Red Feather cut those ropes off us, we followed and waited. We figured you'd end up somewhere and we could help you escape."

"Wait," Greeta said, remembering the events that had led her here. She turned toward Red Feather. "I saw that man throw you off a cliff. I thought you were dead."

"So did we," Nibi said.

"How can you be alive?" Greeta said.

Red Feather shrugged. "I got lucky. There was vegetation at the bottom of the cliff, and it broke my fall. It helped me."

Monz piped up. "He says the plants talked to him."

Greeta shifted her weight from one foot to the other. At any other time in her life she would have been surprised, but the fact she'd spent a good amount of time as a dragon had changed her view of the world. "The plants helped you."

Red Feather nodded. "I spoke to them with the same respect I give any living creature. They gave that respect back to me." He sighed in relief. "But that's a story I can tell another day. I'm happy we can all go home now."

"But I can't," Greeta said.

"Why not?" Nibi said.

Astonished, Greeta didn't understand why she had to explain such an obvious fact to them. "Because I'm not welcome. Because no one wants me there."

"I don't get it," Monz said, turning to his brothers for help. "What is she talking about?"

Frustrated, Greeta said, "You know I loved Wapiti my whole life. I thought he would marry me. That we'd have a family. Now no one wants me. And my own papa sent me away!"

Red Feather snorted. "Wapiti and Animosh are fools. And if you think you're not welcome in your own home, then you're a fool, too." He held out his hand to her, and it reminded her of the way the strange woman in the Dreamtime had held out her scarred hands. "Let's go home."

CHAPTER 37

Together, the brothers and Greeta re-traced their steps through the mountains. They told her how they'd tracked her back to Finehurst's mansion, and she told them most of what had happened after she arrived there, including her discovery of the dragon, the eggs, and the broken eggshells she later found.

"That makes no sense," Nibi said, leading the group along a narrow trail leading down a mountainside to a valley. "Why would he want a dragon? It would be like trying to capture a bear. Why would anyone want to do that?"

"Those are important questions," Greeta said. "If I were still a dragon, I think I might have tried tracking him. Maybe I could have followed him. If I found him, I could learn more." She hesitated. "Maybe that's what I should be doing now, even if I'm not a dragon."

"And what good would that do?" Monz said. "We're all good trackers, and everything we saw points to that man and his people and a dragon going down the cliff to where you saw his ship. The tracks ended there. That means they left on that ship. No one can track a ship."

Nibi said, "And don't say we should have followed the river leading out of the lake. There's only four of us and too many of them."

"And seeing him might have turned you into a dragon again," Monz added.

"But it doesn't feel right, just letting him go like that," Greeta said.

Walking close behind her, Red Feather clapped a solid hand on her shoulder. "That's because you're not a warrior. Why do you think we waited to help you? We watched first. We knew we were outnumbered, and we looked for opportunity. When you became a dragon, you created the distraction we needed." Red Feather shook his head. "If we'd followed the river, we could have been ambushed and killed by them. Or we might have found the ship abandoned and them long gone."

"We could have tracked them after they left the ship," Greeta said.

"No," Red Feather said. "We live for another day when we can be better prepared."

"That's right," Nibi said. "We'll tell the elders what happened. They'll know what to do."

That night they made camp in the valley. While Nibi and Monz snored, Greeta sat next to Red Feather while he stirred the fire. Once again, she thought about what the woman who might be her mother said in the Dreamtime about Greeta's good fortune in being surrounded by people who cared about her.

"When I was a dragon, you said something about my Papa asking you to find me."

Red Feather nodded, stirring the fire with a stick until the flames grew brighter. "He worried about you when Shadow came back and said she'd lost you in the Dreamtime."

His words startled Greeta. Shadow! So

that's what had happened. Somehow going into the Dreamtime must have separated them in the physical world. And Shadow went back to Greeta's village to tell Papa and get help. Shadow hadn't abandoned her, after all. But then a new realization hit Greeta. "You know about the Dreamtime?"

He laughed softly. "Everyone knows about the Dreamtime. It's a place that can clear your head. Give you a better understanding of yourself and your life." He paused. "But it's men who seek it out, not women. I never heard of a woman looking to enter the Dreamtime."

Greeta frowned. "Why?"

Red Feather shrugged. "I never asked."

"Have you been to the Dreamtime?"

"Never needed it."

Greeta absorbed the information for a moment. "Then why did I need it?"

"There has always been something special about you."

Greeta looked at him sharply, wondering if he was ridiculing her until she saw the serious expression in his eyes. "Special?"

Red Feather nodded. "Like I already told

you, Wapiti is a fool. He never noticed how special you are."

A new thought made Greeta shudder. "Please don't tell anyone I became a dragon. Don't ever tell."

Red Feather looked at her as if she'd announced the moon was made of corn. "Why?"

A wave of panic overtook her. "Because they'll send me away again. Because everyone will be afraid of me. Because no one will want to be around me."

"First," Red Feather said, "no one sent you away the first time, and no one will ever send you away. Second, why would anyone be afraid of a shapeshifter?"

Greeta blinked, not sure what she heard. "A what?"

"How can you not know what a shapeshifter is?" Red Feather shook his head and spoke to himself. "How could they have kept you so sheltered in a village our size? Why didn't anyone ever speak of shapeshifting?" He paused and then answered his own question. "Because most people speak of it either with the elders or within their own family."

A bit of flame stirred inside Greeta's

belly, reminding her how she'd felt when she was a dragon. "Would you please tell me what a shapeshifter is?"

"Of course." Red Feather shook himself out of his own thoughts. "A shapeshifter is exactly what it sounds like: someone who can change their own shape. Most shape-shifters change into a deer or a fox or maybe a bear." He grinned. "You're the first one I've heard of who can change into a dragon."

"You're saying that I'm the one who did it." The thought scared Greeta and ex-hilarated her at the same time. "You're saying that somehow I managed to change my mortal shape into the shape of a dragon."

"Yes. And what surprises me is that you would change into an animal you'd never seen before."

"That's not true. I'd seen a dragon that very day. For the first time." Greeta ran her hands over her face, trying to wash away the memory. "The dragon Finehurst held prisoner."

"I see." Red Feather became still.

His stillness scared Greeta, making her feel suddenly alone. "I thought you said people weren't afraid of shapeshifters."

"They're not." Red Feather locked his gaze with hers. "I'm not. I'm just wondering if the reason you changed into a dragon has something to do with seeing one for the first time."

The thought stirred the fire in Greeta's belly. Afraid to face it, she ignored the fire, hoping it would die out on its own. "Is that how shapeshifting works?" A new and welcome distracting thought made her ask, "Are you a shapeshifter?"

Shaking his head, Red Feather said, "Shapeshifters were far more common when our parents were our age. But they've become rare, and no one knows why. No one in our village is a shapeshifter." Red Feather stopped and corrected himself, grinning. "Until now. We have our own shapeshifter."

Greeta allowed herself to feel some hope. "And people won't mind if I'm a shapeshifter?"

"Of course not! Having a shapeshifter in any village is a great gift. An advantage. And even if it weren't, we'd take you back anyway. Even if people were afraid of shapeshifters, it wouldn't matter because you'd be *our* shapeshifter. Just like if you were still a dragon, it wouldn't matter because you'd be *our* dragon." He paused, staring into space. "Everyone is going to be so excited when they see you become a dragon."

Red Feather snapped his fingers. "I almost forgot." He reached into his shoe, withdrew something, and handed it to Greeta. "I found this a little while ago in the courtyard. It must have broken from your neck when you turned into a dragon."

Greeta stared at the pendant Papa had made for her years ago. The dragonfly made of silver, its body the shape of a sword.

CHAPTER 38

Two days later, the brothers and Greeta neared the end of their journey, recognizeing the familiar territory on the outskirts of their village.

Excited, Greeta faced the brothers. "I need to find Papa now and let him know I'm fine." Gesturing toward the shirtless Red Feather and the bare-legged Monz, she said, "I promise I will put on my own clothes and return these to you today." Nodding her thanks, she took off in a bolt and ran as fast as she could toward her village.

Running reminded her of how it had felt to run when she'd been a dragon. Despite her hefty size, she'd easily outrun the boys, racing at a breakneck pace.

And she remembered how running made her feel wild and joyful and free. For the first time as a mortal, she felt the same way now.

Greeta dashed into the far end of her village, happy to see friendly faces, smiling as she ran past them until a familiar voice made her stop.

"Greeta!" Wapiti called out. Running up to her, he embraced her. "I'm sorry. I never meant to hurt you. I need you."

The feelings she'd had for Wapiti all her life came rushing back. She remembered how he'd been her closest friend since childhood. How he'd always been by her side. The plans they'd made for their future.

She returned his embrace until she remembered the way Margreet whispered in her ear when Finehurst had held her the same way. She remembered the way Wapiti had talked to Animosh on the beach. The way he'd let Animosh ridicule her. The way he'd betrayed her.

Greeta pushed him away. If he could have turned so easily on her when she was a mortal, how likely would it have been that he would have stood by her side the way his brothers did when she was a dragon? Greeta decided the answer was that Wapiti would have run the other way, leaving her to fend for herself. Without emotion, she said, "I don't need you. Not anymore." Turning her back on him, she ran, ignoring his pleas for her to come back.

Grinning at the sight of her own home, Greeta burst through the door. "Papa?"

But instead of finding her father, the sight of Shadow tied and bound on the floor shocked Greeta into silence.

Shadow tried to cry out, but a gag muffled her words.

Greeta dashed to the shaman's side, loosening the gag and the ropes that bound her.

"They took your father to the North-lander ship," Shadow said. "You were right. It must have come ashore this morning. Your aunt was here. They took your entire family."

"Finehurst," Greeta said, remembering what Badger Face had told her about how the Northlander man would want to know about her family and where they were. Maybe Badger Face had told him, and now

Finehurst wanted to take them hostage for some reason. Maybe it had something to do with the reason he'd taken the dragon and the eggs hostage. "I have to stop him."

"No," Shadow said. "We should get others to help us."

Greeta scanned her home in search of any kind of weapon. Margreet had taught her to use a sword in the Dreamtime, but the weapons aboard the ship Papa had sailed from the Northlands had been lost when the ship had crashed offshore. She saw nothing that could serve as any kind of weapon. "Go get them," Greeta told Shadow. "I'll go first and stop Finehurst. I'll keep him from leaving until you can bring others to stop him."

Nodding, Shadow ran from the house while Greeta raced through the woods and across the marshlands to the shore. She recognized the Northlander ship the moment she saw it, already casting off from shore while its crew raised the sail. It was the same ship she'd seen on the horizon on the day she'd left her village.

She ran to stand on top of the same dune where she'd spied on Wapiti and Animosh. Waving her arms, she cried out,

"Stop! I'm here! I'm Greeta! I'm the one you want!"

Below, a Northlander bedecked in the finery of furs, silver bracelets up and down both arms, and brightly colored linen clothing stood on the deck and gestured for the sail to be lowered. Moments later, the crew on board rowed the ship back to shore.

Greeta raced down the embankment. By the time she reached the ship, it slid up the beach, and the bedecked man jumped down to meet her.

Astonished, she stopped short.

The man wasn't Finehurst.

"Looky what we got here," the North-lander said. His nose looked so misshapen that it might have been broken with a hammer.

"It be her! The little dragonish daughter of the blacksmiths!" Another man dressed in similar finery jumped onto the sand, his face beaming but his forehead gnarled up in a lump as if it had been struck with a hammer, too.

Startled, Greeta backed away, well aware that they wore long swords at their sides and she had no weapon of any kind.

"Where are my papa and my auntie? What have you done with them?"

The two Northlander men laughed, each circling her from a different side until one stood on her left and the other on her right.

"Trep the blacksmith," the one with the broken nose said. "And Peppa the gatherer of blooms of iron."

Even more startled, Greeta said, "You know them. You know my family."

"Ain't never said we didn't."

The one with the lumpy forehead said, "We be knowing you, as well. And hoping you be as sweet and special as your mother."

More astonished by the moment, Greeta said, "You knew my mother?"

One of them lunged at her, and Greeta backed away only to find the other one scooping her over his shoulder and hauling her onto the ship.

"Say farewell to all you know, Dragon Girl," the lumpy one said.

Greeta struggled but couldn't free herself from him. She watched in horror as the other one shoved the ship back into the water, hopped on board, and commanded the crew to row again. In moments, the ship sped out to sea, too far for any of the villagers who now ran onto the beach to do anything but watch it head East.

Finding herself dropped to the floorboards of the deck, Greeta searched frantically but saw no signs of her father or aunt. She cried out when rough, weathered hands held her in place.

"There, there, my pretty pony of a dragonish girl," the lumpy one said. "You have nothing to worry about. The best adventures are yet to come."

Greeta closed her eyes, wishing herself to become a dragon so she could stop this man, scoop her loved ones up in her jaws, and swim back to shore with them. She wished as hard as she could, trying to stir up fire in her belly.

But no flame would spark into existence.

Terrified, Greeta stared at her mortal body, weak and useless.

"Ain't that peculiar," the one with the broken nose said. "She ain't got it figured out yet."

The other one beamed, holding out an

open palm. "Then I win. Didn't I tell you she be just like her mama? Pay up."

With a dark grimace, the one with the broken nose yanked a large silver bracelet from his forearm and smacked it into the other's hand.

Confused, Greeta stared at them, wondering by all the spirits of the Great Turtle Lands and the Northlands, where these men would take her and why they had abducted her family.

"Greeta!"

Looking up, she cried in relief. "Papa!"

When he wrapped his arms around her, Greeta cried, happy to be back in his embrace. Moments later, she recognized more gentle arms around them both. Backing away, Greeta said, "Auntie Peppa!" Lowering her voice, she said, "We have to figure out how to escape."

But Auntie Peppa frowned and said, "Why?"

Papa shook hands with the men who had hauled her on board.

"I'm very confused," Greeta said. "Shadow said they abducted you."

"That be true," the lumpy one said. "Until we got them to the ship, got talking, and found out we could work together."

"They promised they'd help us find you," Papa said, holding Greeta close. "But you found us instead."

"So why aren't we going home now?" Greeta said, more puzzled by the moment.

"Because they're friends," Auntie Peppa said. "And we promised to help them in return."

Greeta looked at the two Northlander men, thinking they must be very strange friends to first abduct people and then decide to join forces with them. She gazed back to the shore of the only home she had ever known, missing it already. Staring, she realized she was searching for Red Feather and disappointed not to see him there. "But we'll be coming back home?"

"Of course," Papa said.

A new thought struck Greeta, and she pointed at the lumpy man. "Why does he call me a dragonish girl?"

Papa sighed and exchanged a worried look with Auntie Peppa.

But the lumpy man piped up and said, "Because I be knowing you since you was a little one freshly hatched out of your shell."

Shocked, Greeta faced her family, but neither Papa nor Auntie Peppa could look her in the eye, leaving her torn between the relief of finding them safe and sound and the dismay that they'd never told her that she was anything but mortal.

Steadying herself, Greeta said, "I imagine we have a long journey ahead of us, and plenty of time for you to tell me the truth about who I really am."

ABOUT THE AUTHOR

When Resa Nelson's short story "The Dragonslayer's Sword" was first published in *Science Fiction Age* magazine, it ranked 2nd in that magazine's first Readers Top Ten poll. Around the same time, the manager of a major bookstore contacted the magazine editor asking how to buy the novel because many of his customers were asking to buy it.

No such novel existed. Only the short story existed. Readers assumed it had come from a novel.

This is when Resa realized all her readers are smarter than she is, because they knew there was more to the story. It only took her eight years to figure out what they already knew. She plans to write at least four series that take place in her Dragonslayer World. Series #1 (Dragonslayer Series) is complete. *Dragonfly* is Book 1 in the Dragonfly series.

Visit Resa's website at www.resanelson.com and follow her on Twitter at @ResaNelson.